ABOUT THE ALDEN ALL STARS

Nothing's more important to Derrick, Matt, Josh, and Jesse than their team, the Alden Panthers. Whether the sport is football, hockey, baseball, or track-and-field, the four seventh-graders can always be found practicing, sweating, and giving their all. Sometimes the Panthers are on their way to a winning season, and sometimes the team can't do anything right. But no matter what, you can be sure the Alden All Stars are playing to win.

"This fast-paced [series] is sure to be a hit with young readers."   —*Publishers Weekly*

"Packed with play-by-play action and snappy dialogue, the text adeptly captures the seventh-grade sports scene."   —*ALA Booklist*

The *Alden All Stars* series:

Blindside Blitz

David Halecroft

PUFFIN BOOKS

PUFFIN BOOKS
Published by the Penguin Group
Viking Penguin, a division of Penguin Books USA Inc.,
375 Hudson Street, New York, New York 10014, U.S.A.
Penguin Books Ltd, 27 Wrights Lane, London W8 5TZ, England
Penguin Books Australia Ltd, Ringwood, Victoria, Australia
Penguin Books Canada Ltd, 10 Alcorn Avenue, Ontario, Canada M4V 3B2
Penguin Books (N.Z.) Ltd, 182–190 Wairau Road, Auckland 10, New Zealand

Penguin Books Ltd, Registered Offices: Harmondsworth, Middlesex, England

First published in Puffin Books, 1991
1   3   5   7   9   10   8   6   4   2
Copyright © Daniel Weiss and Associates, 1991
All rights reserved

Library of Congress Catalog Card Number: 91-53027
ISBN 0-14-034906-5

Printed in the United States of America
Set in Century Schoolbook

Blindside Blitz

1

Matt Greene took a deep breath, crouched down at the thirty-yard line, and listened for the quarterback's signal. He knew he had to score a touchdown on this play, and his brown eyes stared like laser beams at the end zone.

"Hut, hut, hut!"

Matt burst forward, looking for holes in the defense. At the twenty-yard line, he faked right, cut left, and ran full speed for the pass. As long as Jesse

Kissler threw the ball exactly right—hard and high—Matt knew he had a chance of scoring a touchdown, and winning the bet.

"I'll have my pizza with pepperoni and extra cheese," Josh Bank shouted as he ran. "And peppers!"

"You haven't won yet!" Matt yelled, looking back over his shoulder for the pass.

Matt knew it was a crazy bet. He and Jesse had to score a touchdown from the thirty-yard line— against two rushers and five pass defenders. If they didn't score in one play, they had to buy pizzas for the defense after practice. If they *did* score, Matt and Jesse could order whatever they wanted at Pete's Pizza.

Jesse's arm snapped back and released a beautiful clothesline pass, fast and straight as a bullet. The ball was high, and sped toward Matt in a perfect spiral. Matt and two defensemen leapt into the air, reaching their hands up for the ball. Matt soared high above the others, though, and snatched the pass out of midair.

He landed with the ball on the fifteen-yard line, and tucked it into his side. Duke Duquette tried to grab him around the legs, but Matt spun off the tackle, jumped over Duke, and sprinted toward the end zone.

Josh and Russell Shultz charged forward, trying to angle Matt into the sideline. Matt gave a head fake, changed direction, and left both defenders in the dust. They could only stand and watch as Matt crossed into the end zone all alone.

"Yeah!" Matt shouted, lifting his arms. "Touchdown!" He spiked the ball and did his touchdown dance—a set of top-speed stutter-steps. Then he ran up to Josh and smacked his friend playfully on the shoulder pads.

"Hey, Josh," Matt said. "I think I'll have that pizza with pepperoni and extra cheese. And a meatball hoagie, too. And a large soda, and maybe a—"

"Okay, okay," Josh said, laughing. "You guys won the bet."

It was two weeks before the start of school, and Alden Junior High's eighth-grade football team was waiting for the first summer practice to begin. Football was Matt Greene's favorite sport, and even though he was hot beneath the summer sun, he felt great in pads again. Matt liked playing baseball and basketball, but running around a baseball diamond or a basketball court was nothing compared to the thrill he felt when he ran down a football field. Matt loved to crash through holes in the defense, block linebackers, break tackles, and score big touchdowns.

"Okay, men," Coach Litzinger called as he walked onto the field. "Let's get this season off on the right foot."

All the players gathered in a huddle around Coach. The word around school was that Coach Litzinger worked his players hard—harder than the seventh-grade coach. That was okay by Matt. He was ready for anything Coach Litzinger wanted to throw his way.

All of a sudden, Coach spun around and whipped a ball right at Matt's stomach. Matt was so surprised that he didn't have time to react, and the ball bounced off him and fell to the ground.

"Welcome to the eighth-grade Panthers," Coach laughed, as he turned to the rest of the team. "I want everyone to learn the most important lesson in football. Always be one hundred percent alert. Every game is won on a couple of big plays. The problem is, nobody knows when those plays are going to happen. So everyone on the Panthers has to play heads-up ball. Got it?"

Coach whipped another ball right at Matt. This time Matt caught it one-handed. He smiled and tossed the ball back. Matt could tell he was going to like Coach Litzinger.

"We can have a good team this year," Coach went on. "But it will take hard work. Everybody's got to know their job, and do it well." Coach walked out onto the grass. "Okay, men, spread out across the field in three rows. We're going to start off with some agility drills."

The team lined up and Coach had them run sideways for twenty yards. The players kept their arms in front of them, their eyes straight ahead, and crossed one leg over the other. They kept going from side to side, until they were huffing and puffing. Then Coach had them run backward, reaching back for long strides and raising their knees up as high as they could.

Matt was in the line behind Jesse's and he could see his friend struggling with the drills. Jesse was a tall boy with sandy blond hair, blue eyes, and a great arm. He had led the Panthers baseball team to the state championship with his expert pitching, and he could hurl the football just as well. Still, he was clumsy on his feet, and sometimes his legs got tangled up.

"You know what?" Jesse said, as they finished up the drills. "I wish I could run like you."

"You don't have to be a good runner to be a good quarterback," Matt answered. "As long as you can pass the ball, you'll do great."

"I guess so," Jesse answered.

"Just leave the running to me," Matt said. "And I'll leave the passing to you."

Coach blew his whistle and called the team to the blocking dummies. Matt liked blocking. It was an important part of being a running back. Lots of plays called for him to run in front of the other running back, throwing solid blocks.

Coach blew the whistle and Matt ran forward. He kept his back straight, and drove his shoulder into the big blue pad. Working his legs hard to get all the power he could, Matt pushed the dummy along the grass. It felt great to be back on the football field.

"You're doing some mean hitting out there," Josh said to Matt at the break. "You looked more like a lineman than a running back."

"I'm not scared of hitting," Matt answered. "I figure if I'm supposed to block, I'd better do it right. You can't be scared of mixing it up."

"Quarterbacks are different," Jesse said. "We have to protect ourselves. If the first-string quarterback gets injured, then the whole team can fall apart."

"So you think that quarterbacks are more important than running backs?" Matt said, lifting his eyebrows playfully.

"Definitely," Jesse answered with a smile.

"Forget it," Matt said. "Anybody can throw a ball or hand a ball off. How many people can dodge and jump and run? Besides, running backs score the most touchdowns."

Jesse opened his mouth to answer, but Coach Litzinger blew his whistle and called the team over to the field.

"We'll settle this later," Jesse whispered to Matt.

Coach walked the boys through a simple screen-pass play, showing the offensive line how to pull, and the defensive line how to attack. Matt was supposed to line up in the fullback position, directly behind Jesse. On the snap, Matt was to swing out to his right, cross the line of scrimmage, and catch the screen pass.

"Okay, men," Coach said. "Let's run it, nice and easy."

Matt's heart was pounding as he got down in the three point stance.

"Hut, hut, hut!"

Matt rushed forward, then cut to his right as Jesse faded back. He crossed the line of scrimmage and looked behind him for the ball. He could see that the defense had broken through, and that Jesse was in trouble. Just as Jesse took his arm back to throw, he was hit by a defensive lineman and tackled.

Coach blew his whistle.

"Okay, listen up," Coach began angrily. "Never tackle your own quarterback when he's about to pass. That's the easiest way to injure a quarterback's arm. The last thing we want to do is injure Jesse. You'll be able to hit as hard as you want when we scrimmage with Williamsport next week."

Even though he knew it made sense, Matt didn't like to lay off in practice. It just wasn't as much fun as playing good hard football. He could hardly wait until the scrimmage against Williamsport, when he'd really be able to hit.

"Did you hear what Coach said about injuring a quarterback's arm?" Jesse said to Matt later that afternoon at Pete's Pizza. "I guess that proves which position is the most important."

"All I said was that the quarterback doesn't get in the action as much as the running back," Matt answered, as he looked up at the menu. "It just seems kind of boring."

"What!" Jesse said with a laugh. "The quarterback

creates the action. It's not that easy to throw the ball exactly on target."

"It sounds pretty easy to me," Matt said. The two friends had this argument a lot. The truth was, Matt thought being a quarterback was a breeze—at least compared to being a running back.

"Why don't you two shut up and order," Josh said. "Otherwise, you won't collect on your bet."

"Okay," Matt said, grinning as he and Jesse strolled up to the counter. "Let's chow down."

2

Matt was psyched when he saw the team roster a few days later. Now it was official: Matt was the first-string running back of the Panthers. Jesse was listed as the quarterback, Josh as wide receiver, and Russell Shultz as the other running back. Dave McShea and Duke Duquette were rotating receivers, responsible for delivering the plays from Coach to Jesse.

The offensive linemen were Jeremy Blumenthal, A.J. Pape, Paul Sansone, and Lefty Lugar, with Bruce Judge at center. The defense was headed up by Chip Simon at middle linebacker, the biggest guy on the Panthers. The defensive linemen were Vin Rossi, Jeff Hancher, Donny Fields, and Delmar Jefferson.

The Panthers practiced fiercely in preparation for the scrimmage against Williamsport. Matt and Jesse worked overtime on their hand-offs. They also practiced the fake hand-off, which was a key part of the play-action pass. So when the Williamsport bus pulled into the parking lot the next week, the Panthers were ready for action.

"It takes guts for a running back to run the play action," Jesse said to Matt, as they walked onto the field for the scrimmage. "You get creamed and you don't even have the ball."

"Yeah," Josh added, ramming Matt with his helmet. "What a bummer."

"It's my job," Matt said, laughing as he rammed Josh back. "Besides, it's kind of fun getting a fake hand-off, and trying to fake the defense out."

"And if you do it right," Jesse said, "it gives *me* more time to get the pass off."

"I don't mind getting tackled anyway," Matt said.

"Really?" Josh answered with a sly smile. "When I play football, I try *not* to get tackled."

11

"Very funny," Matt said, knocking his shoulder pads into Josh's chest. "You know what I mean."

"Speaking of tackles . . ." Jesse said, pointing toward the Williamsport team.

Matt saw who Jesse was pointing at, and stopped in his tracks. The guy was wearing number sixty-six, and he was way bigger than all the other Williamsport players. Matt watched number sixty-six hit the blocking dummy, growling as he charged. Matt gulped. There was no doubt, the guy looked mean.

"I've heard about number sixty-six," Josh said, as the three friends started walking again. "He plays middle linebacker. His name is Anderson, and I hear he likes to blitz."

"He likes to blitz?" Jesse said, knitting his brow.

Matt knew why Jesse was worried. Even Matt's heart skipped a beat whenever he saw linebackers charging across the line of scrimmage in a blitz. But the blitz was especially hard during pass plays, because the quarterback doesn't have time to throw a good pass. And since Jesse was too slow to be a good scrambler, a blitzing defense had a good chance of scoring a sack.

"Don't worry, Jesse," Matt said. "He can't be *that* mean."

"Oh, yes he can," Josh added, slipping his helmet over his mop of bright red hair. "That's why the wide receiver is the best position on the team. Since we're always running upfield, we don't have to worry about the blitz. Just think about the great ones, like Jerry Rice and . . ."

"Okay, okay, Mr. Jerry Rice," a deep voice said behind them. When the boys turned around, they saw Coach Litzinger.

"Let's keep our minds on the scrimmage, men," Coach said, as the team gathered around him on the sideline. "Remember what I said in the locker room last week. Stay alert, one hundred percent of the time. Williamsport is a tough team, but we can take them. All right, Panthers, let's go!"

The Williamsport defense turned out to be as tough as they looked. Everywhere Matt tried to run, he seemed to collide into Anderson and his big number sixty-six. But the Panthers' defense was playing well, too, and the first quarter ended scoreless.

In the second quarter, Matt decided that things had to change. Anderson or no Anderson, the Panthers needed a touchdown.

On the next set of downs, the Panthers started from their own forty-five-yard line. On three, Matt charged to his left and Jesse faded back. Jesse pitched out, and Matt kept his eyes on the ball until it reached his hands. Then he tucked it under his arm, and sprinted toward a hole in the defense.

Russell made a great block, and Matt jumped over the tackled players like a hurdler. He gave a head fake to one defenseman, then cut the other way and broke through a tackle.

Out of the corner of his eye, Matt saw a Williamsport safety barreling toward him. He did a quick stutter-step and dodged right around the diving player. Now there was nothing but open field between Matt and a touchdown. He turned on the speed and pumped his arms.

Suddenly Matt felt someone grab him around the shoulders from behind and drag him to the ground. A huge weight fell on top of him and knocked his wind out, but Matt somehow kept hold of the ball. As he was trying to catch his breath, Matt looked up and saw Anderson standing above him, laughing.

"You think you're hot, don't you?" Anderson said, as he turned to jog back to his huddle. "Well you guys don't stand a chance against me. Not a chance in the world."

Matt didn't say a word. He just wanted to get the ball again, and show Anderson that he wasn't scared. The next call was a play-action pass. Jesse was supposed to fake the hand-off to Matt, and then throw to Josh near the goal line.

On two, Matt charged forward, holding his arms as if he were getting a hand-off—but before he took another step, he saw that the defense was blitzing. The Williamsport linebackers had broken through the line, and were heading right for Matt and Jesse.

Jesse turned around and stuffed the ball into Matt's stomach, then he pulled it out at the last second. Matt kept running forward as if he had the ball. Nobody was fooled by the play action and Anderson ran right by him. Jesse tried to scramble, but Anderson was on him in a flash. Just as Anderson creamed him into the grass, Jesse managed to chuck a long pass downfield.

Matt watched the pass sail through the air. It was a perfect spiral, and it was heading right for Josh's arms. Josh leaped for the ball and caught it in midair—then landed in the end zone for the first Panther touchdown.

"Yes!" Matt shouted as he ran over to Jesse. "Amazing throw!"

He gave Jesse a hand and pulled him to his feet.

"That Anderson guy sure hits hard," Jesse said, as they headed toward the sideline.

At the end of the second quarter Williamsport scored a touchdown on a long pass to a wide receiver. The score was Alden 7, Williamsport 7, and when the fourth quarter began, the game was still tied.

The Panthers were on a good drive, and had moved the ball all the way to Williamsport's thirty-five-yard line. It was second down and ten, and Matt was supposed to go left for a screen pass.

"Hut, hut!" Jesse cried.

Matt broke left, crossed the line of scrimmage, and looked back for Jesse's pass. He saw Jesse throw the ball, and then a second later he saw Anderson slam Jesse to the ground and land on top of him.

Matt was looking so intently at Jesse, that he almost missed the pass. Luckily, the pass was picture perfect, and all Matt had to do was open up his arms and catch it.

Matt tucked the ball in, changed direction, dodged around a safety, then sprinted toward the corner of the end zone. He looked behind him and saw two defenders sprinting after him. That's when he turned on the speed. A few seconds later he crossed the goal line—but this time he didn't do his touchdown dance. Instead, he dashed upfield to see if Jesse was okay.

Jesse was lying on the ground, surrounded by

Coach and the rest of the Panthers. As soon as he saw Jesse's face, Matt knew Jesse was hurt.

"What's wrong?" Matt asked Coach Litzinger, who was kneeling next to Jesse.

"It's his ankle," Coach said. "It might be broken."

"I can't believe they didn't call a penalty on Anderson," Jesse said, blinking back the tears. "That was definitely a late hit."

"Don't worry about that now," Coach said, lifting Jesse up. "Let's just get you to the hospital."

Matt couldn't believe what Anderson had done. A late hit wasn't only illegal, it was downright dangerous. Matt saw Anderson standing by his teammates, and ran over to him.

"You're a jerk," Matt said, giving Anderson a push. "You probably broke Jesse's ankle."

"Don't mess with me," Anderson said. "Football's a tough game. I hit your quarterback fair and square."

"Fair and square?" Matt yelled, giving Anderson another push. "It was a late hit and you know it."

Anderson shoved Matt, and Matt took his arm back to throw a punch—but the referee stepped in and broke them up. The two opponents glared at each other, then Matt turned around and headed toward the sideline.

The Panthers decided to try for the extra point instead of the two-point conversion. Duke was the kicker, and he booted the ball soccer-style. He was usually pretty good, but this time the kick sailed wide of the goal posts. The score was Alden 13, Williamsport 7.

One of the parents at the game took Jesse to the hospital, and Russell Shultz went in as quarterback. Russell's hand-offs weren't very good, and Matt fumbled twice. On the second fumble, a Williamsport player recovered the ball and ran it all the way for a touchdown. When Williamsport scored the extra point, the Panthers were suddenly down by a score of 14–13.

For the rest of the quarter, Russell couldn't even get the Panthers close enough for a field-goal attempt. With Jesse out of the game, the Panthers just seemed to fall apart. When the whistle blew, signaling the end of the game, Alden had lost by one point.

After showering and changing, Matt jumped on his bike and sped to the Cranbrook Hospital. He couldn't believe they had lost to Williamsport, and he hoped that Jesse was okay and that he would be able to come back soon. If Russell stayed at quarterback, Matt knew that the Panthers would have a rough season.

Jesse was lying in a small white room, wearing a cast that came all the way up to his knee.

"Oh, no," Matt said, as soon as he saw the cast. "I don't believe it."

"You better believe it," Jesse answered sadly, turning his head on the pillow. "My ankle's fractured, and the doctors say I may miss the whole season."

"You mean we have to play with Russell as quarterback?" Matt said, taking a seat by the bed.

"No," Jesse said. "I guess Coach Litzinger raced over here right after the game and didn't tell you the news."

"Tell me what?" Matt asked, suddenly worried.

Jesse frowned. "Coach said he spoke to Russell and Russell understands," Jesse began. "He . . ."

"What?" Jesse asked. "Just tell me."

"Coach wants *you* to be quarterback," Jesse answered.

"*Me?*" Matt cried, springing to his feet. "Quarterback?"

3

When Matt left Jesse's hospital room that afternoon, he felt like his whole season had been wrecked.
Running back was the only position he had ever
wanted to play. His heroes were Bo Jackson and
Barry Sanders. Even Matt's father, Big Bill Greene,
had been a running back in the NFL. Ever since
Matt was small, his father had been teaching him
how to run, fake, and think like a running back.

"Why can't Russell play quarterback? He'll get

better," Matt grumbled to himself, as he climbed onto his bike. "Why do *I* have to ruin my entire season, just because Jesse got hurt?"

Matt turned his bike onto Patch Street, zoomed down a big hill, and coasted into downtown Cranbrook. Some of the leaves had begun to turn yellow on the big maple trees in Danahy Park, and Matt was a little chilly by the time he stopped in front of Big Bill's Goal Post. Football weather was definitely on its way.

The walls at the restaurant, which was owned by Matt's father, were covered with old football photographs, the floor was carpeted with Astro-Turf, and all the waiters wore referee uniforms.

"Hi, son," Mr. Greene said, when he saw Matt come in. "How did the game go?"

"We lost," Matt said.

"That's too bad. But it was only a scrimmage."

Matt shrugged and looked down at the floor.

"Is something else wrong?" Mr. Greene asked.

He led Matt to a booth in the corner, and then Matt told him everything: how a jerk named Anderson tackled Jesse, how Jesse's ankle was fractured, and how Coach Litzinger wanted *him* to play quarterback.

"I know you were looking forward to being a running back this season," Mr. Greene said. "But quarterback isn't so bad."

"It's not running back," Matt answered. "You almost never get to score touchdowns when you play quarterback. And it looks so dull."

"Well, Matt," Mr. Greene said with a laugh, as he stood up to greet some guests. "Maybe it won't be as boring as you think."

The next day was the first day of school. It was also the first day that Matt was officially the Panthers' quarterback. That gave Matt two good reasons to be in a rotten mood.

Before practice that afternoon, Matt asked Coach why Russell couldn't be quarterback instead.

"Because I think you'll do a better job," Coach said. "You're the best natural athlete on the team. And without a strong quarterback, we'll lose every game. Russell is a little disappointed, but even he agrees we need you as QB. Now let's get to work. You've got a lot to learn."

Coach blew his whistle and the team gathered around him at the thirty-yard line.

"We played a good scrimmage yesterday," Coach

said, looking at his clipboard. "Football is a rough game, and injuries happen. Every team has to learn how to keep its spirit up, and play its best game— even when one of its key players is off the field."

Everyone looked over to Jesse, who was sitting on the bench with his crutches. His big white cast stuck out in front of him.

"As you all know by now, Matt is going to be our new quarterback," Coach went on. "I expect everyone to get behind him. We play our first conference game in two days. That only gives us two practices to break Matt in."

After warming up, the team got ready to run scrimmage plays. Coach reminded everyone to run the plays at half speed, and to be careful not to hit anyone too hard. The first play Coach called was a simple hand-off to Russell.

The offensive line got into position, and Matt strolled up to Bruce Judge, the center. He bent his knees, and put his hands in position for the snap. All he had to do was hand the ball to Russell, and then sit back and watch the play.

"Ready," Matt said, in a quiet voice. "Hut, hut . . . hut!"

By the time Matt called out his third hut, most of

the offensive line had jumped offside. Bruce snapped the ball back into Matt's hands, where it jammed into Matt's fingers and fell to the ground.

Russell was charging forward for the hand-off, and Matt could see the defense crashing toward him through the line. In a panic, he picked up the ball and slammed it into Russell's stomach so hard that Russell doubled over on the ground. The loose ball bounced to the side, and a defenseman recovered it for a turnover.

Coach blew his whistle.

"Well, where do you want me to start?" Coach said, looking at Matt. Some of the boys laughed, and Matt felt his face burn with embarrassment. He could tell that Coach wasn't mad at him, but still he had wanted to do well on his first play.

"First, you can't whisper the snap count—you've got to shout it out, loud and strong," Coach began. "Second, the cadence on your count was all off. That's what made the linemen jump offside. In a game, that would have cost us yardage. Third, you didn't put your hands in the correct position for the snap. That's why the ball dropped. Fourth, you looked at the defense charging in, and that made you miss your target for the hand-off. And last, but not least, you slammed the ball so hard into your running back that he fumbled the ball for a turnover."

"I didn't ask to be quarterback," Matt said, under his breath. He looked over to Jesse on the sidelines, and saw that Jesse was trying hard not to laugh. Maybe this quarterback stuff wasn't as easy as Matt thought.

"Okay," Coach said, taking a deep breath. "Let's take it one step at a time. The count begins the play. If a team can't get the snap right, they might as well hang up their helmets and take up golf."

The offense lined up beside Matt, holding their hands about a foot apart. Matt called the snap signal, and instead of charging ahead, the offense clapped their hands. At first, everyone clapped at a different time. But soon the team got used to Matt's call, and everyone started clapping together.

"Now that we've got that down," Coach told Matt, "We've got to work on the snap itself, so you don't fumble it anymore."

Bruce Judge, the Panthers' center, squatted down and got ready for the snap. Matt walked up and put his hands in position.

"Stop right there!" Coach called. "You've got to place your hands so that the center can feel exactly where he's supposed to snap the ball. Keep your thumbs together, and turn your hands to the left. That way, the ball will be snapped into your throwing hand—and the laces will be right across your fingers, where you want them."

Matt adjusted the position of his hands, then called the starting count. Bruce snapped the ball and it fell out of Matt's hands again.

"You moved," Bruce said. "You've got to keep your hands still until you've got the ball."

Matt and Bruce practiced the snap again and again. Matt was starting to get worried about being quarterback. It seemed like there was so much to learn, especially with the first game of the season just two days away.

During the water break, Jesse hobbled up to Matt.

"Having fun?" Jesse asked.

"Sure," Matt answered. "I haven't had this much fun since I went to the dentist to get a cavity filled."

"The important thing about quarterback," Jesse said, "is keeping your cool. It's like pitching in baseball. Just go out there, relax, and get the job done."

Coach blew his whistle to signal the end of break.

"We'd better work on the hand-off next," Coach said. "Now you don't want to slam the ball into your running back's gut. Just pretend that the football is an egg. You don't want to break an egg all over Russell, do you?"

Matt laughed and shook his head.

"Good," Coach went on. "Aim for Russell's far hip pad, and put the ball there nice and soft."

The offense and defense lined up. Matt put his hands in position, called the starting count in a loud voice, and the Panthers burst into action. Matt felt the ball snap into his hands, with the laces laid across his fingers. He turned and ran back, holding the ball out for Russell—but then he noticed the defense rushing in and lost sight of Russell's far hip pad. He ended up slamming the ball into Russell's elbow, and causing him to fumble again.

Coach blew his whistle.

"You're still thinking like a running back, Matt," Coach said. "When you play running back, you always keep your eyes on the defense, right? That way you can find the holes and run through them. When you're *giving* a hand-off, you should never look at the defense. It's hard to do, since they'll be charging in and trying to cream you. But you've got to keep your eyes on the running back's far hip pad, or else you'll miss the target. Let's try it again."

The Panthers had a long practice that day, and by the end of it Matt was totally exhausted. After he changed and showered in the locker room, he walked outside and found Jesse waiting for him.

"I guess playing quarterback isn't as easy as I thought it would be," Matt admitted, as the two friends walked slowly down the street. "Why did you have to fracture your stupid ankle?"

"I didn't *mean* to," Jesse answered. "Besides, it was Anderson's fault."

"Yeah," Matt said. "I can't wait to play Williamsport again. I'm going to show Anderson a thing or two."

"Hey," Jesse said. "Why don't you be the first person to sign my cast?"

Jesse held out a red magic marker. Matt took it, knelt down, and wrote on Jesse's cast in big red letters: MATT GREENE—RUNNING BACK.

4

"Okay, men," Coach Litzinger shouted, clapping his hands. "That's enough warm-up. Let's get to work on some plays."

It was the next day at practice, and the Panthers had just finished their last set of backward runs. Matt was bummed out that the warm-ups were ending so soon. Now he'd have to be a quarterback again.

"We're going to work on pitch-outs and pass plays," Coach said. "We'll get to see what kind of arm our new quarterback has."

Matt had always had a good arm. In fact, if there was one part of being a quarterback that Matt was sure he could handle, it was passing. He knew how to lead a runner with the throw, so that the ball would land right in the runner's arms.

The first play Coach wanted was a simple flag-pattern pass to Josh. Matt knew what to expect. Josh would come off the line of scrimmage at about half-speed, then break full speed toward the flag at the corner of the end zone. Matt's job was to get the ball to Josh *before* Josh ran out of bounds. It seemed easy enough.

The offense and defense lined up on the field, and Matt got ready for the snap.

"Ready!" he shouted, in a loud voice. "Hut, hut!"

Matt felt the ball snap into his hands, and watched the front line charge forward. He faded back into the pocket, then saw Josh break to his right, get behind the defender, and sprint full speed toward the flag. Matt put his fingers across the laces and got ready to throw. He pumped the ball a few times, waiting for Josh to turn around and look for the pass.

But Josh *didn't* turn around. He just kept running.

Finally Josh glanced over his shoulder—and Matt chucked the ball as fast and hard as he could. By the time the ball came down, Josh was already three steps out of bounds.

"It was a good throw, just too late," Coach said, tossing another football to Matt. "You're a receiver, Matt. You know that the receiver doesn't look for the ball until *after* the ball has been thrown. That means the quarterback has to know exactly when and where to throw the ball."

"I know," Matt said. "It just feels strange to throw the ball when the receiver isn't even looking."

"That's why the pass has to be perfectly timed," Josh said, still breathing hard from his running. "On the flag play, I count to five in my head. When I get to four, I figure that you just threw the ball. When I get to five, I look for the pass."

"So *I* should count to five, too," Matt said, knitting his brow.

"That's right," Coach said. "Now you and Josh work on the flag play until you get it right."

Matt got the snap, faded back, and started counting to five in his head, while Josh ran forward at half-speed, then broke toward the flag in a sprint. When he counted to four, Matt threw the pass. His arm felt good, and the ball went speeding right toward the target.

Matt waited for Josh to turn around—but Josh didn't, and the pass sped closer and closer.

The ball hit Josh in the back of the helmet, and he fell forward on his face. Matt couldn't help laughing.

"Why didn't you turn around and look for the ball?" Matt yelled to Josh. "The throw was perfect."

"You threw the pass too soon," Josh answered. "You must have counted too fast."

The next time the team tried the play, Matt and Josh had their timing down. Matt threw the ball at just the right time and Josh turned around to catch it. But the pass defender was covering Josh tight, and he jumped up and snagged the ball. Matt slapped his leg in frustration.

"Okay, let's take a break," Coach said, putting his arm around Matt's shoulder pads. "I know you've got a lot to remember. Just relax, and do the best you can."

Matt walked over to Jesse, who was sitting on the sideline with his cast up on the bench. Plopping himself down next to his friend, he took off his helmet, and put his head in his hands.

"I don't want to be a quarterback," Matt said, feeling depressed. "I've already thrown my first interception."

"Don't worry," Jesse said. "I'll tell you how to avoid interceptions. Keep your eyes on the pass defender, not the receiver. You *know* where the receiver is going to be, right? But you don't know where the pass defender is going to be. If the defender is too close, you look for your secondary receiver."

"Okay," Matt said. "That's one more thing I have to remember."

After break, Coach talked to Matt about automatics. Matt knew how to run automatics from the running back position. Whenever a quarterback called out an automatic, Matt knew he was supposed to forget about the play they had planned in the huddle, and run the automatic play instead.

Now that Matt was the quarterback, *he* had to call out the automatic. It was even more stuff that Matt might mess up.

The Panthers only had two automatics—a quarterback option to the left, and a hand-off to the right. The signal for the quarterback option was "Green 53," and the signal for the hand-off was "Green 18."

"I know the signals, Coach," Matt said. "But when am I supposed to call an automatic?"

"It's easy," Coach answered, drawing a diagram full of circles and arrows on his clipboard. "Let's say you're planning to run a pitch-out to the right, okay?

But when you set up on the line of scrimmage, you notice that the defense has set up strong on the right side. If you run the pitch-out to the right, the defense will kill you. So you call for the quarterback option to the *left*—Green 53. That way you'll be able to run around the defense, and gain some big yardage."

Matt understood what Coach was saying. It seemed pretty easy. If the defense was setting up heavy on the left, you called the automatic to the right. If they were setting up heavy on the right, you called the automatic to the left.

"Now make sure you know the signals, Matt," Coach said. "Or else you could really screw things up in the game tomorrow."

"Green 53—that's the quarterback option to the left," Matt said. "Green 18—that's the hand-off to the right."

"You got it," Coach said. "Now remember to call them out loud and clear. Everybody needs to hear that the play is being changed. Now let's try one on the field."

The offense was supposed to run a pitch-out to the right. Matt called the play in the huddle, and the team jogged up to the line of scrimmage. As Matt got his hands ready for the snap, he looked at the defense. They were definitely set up strong on the right side, exactly where Russell was supposed to run with the pitch-out. Matt knew that he should call the quarterback-option automatic, because it went to the left.

"Ready, Green 53," Matt called out in a loud voice.

The quarterback option was Matt's favorite play. He and Russell would run along together, and Matt had the choice of either pitching to Russell or running with the ball himself.

There wasn't much question what Matt wanted to do. He couldn't wait to run with the ball.

"Hut, hut, hut!"

Matt got the snap and faded back a few steps, then broke to his left, with Russell keeping just behind him. It felt great to be running with the ball again, and not thinking about calling plays. He smiled as he gave a head fake, and cut sharply across the line of scrimmage.

Matt broke one tackle, spun out of another, jumped around his blocker, and sprinted toward the end zone. Playing quarterback would be a breeze if only he could run with the ball on every play. Matt crossed the goal line for a touchdown, then did his famous stutter-step touchdown dance.

He just hoped he had a chance to do the dance in the opening game the next day.

———

After practice, Matt walked over to Jesse's house to help Jesse with his training. Jesse had some barbells in his basement, and a weight machine that he used to exercise his legs.

"I talked to the doctor today," Jesse said, curling the barbell. The muscle in his arm was bulging. "He said that I may be able to come back for a few games this season."

"That would be great," Matt said. "The sooner you come back, the better."

"I can't believe I'm going to miss so many games," Jesse said, putting the weight down and mopping his brow. "I really liked being the quarterback of the Panthers."

"As far as I'm concerned, you still *are* the quarterback of the Panthers," Matt answered. "And I'm still the running back."

5

"Let me have your potato chips," Bannister said, pointing to Matt's bag in the cafeteria of Alden Junior High the next day. "You haven't even touched them."

"They're all yours," Matt answered, tossing the bag across the lunchroom table. "Not that you *need* any more potato chips."

Bannister was overweight and took a lot of kidding from his friends because of it. He didn't mind too much, though. His weight didn't stop him from participating in track and field events, and from playing on the hockey team. Besides, he loved to joke around, too.

"How about your sandwich?" Bannister asked, after he had cleaned up Matt's chips.

Matt didn't answer. On a regular day, he would have been the one scrounging for potato chips. He was usually the first one to finish his lunch, too, and the first one to hit the line for an ice cream bar. But this afternoon Matt wasn't feeling hungry at all. He was way too nervous to eat. He tossed his sandwich across the table, where Bannister caught it with a smile.

"Mmmm," Bannister said, making a funny face. "Meatloaf, my favorite."

Derrick Larson was sitting next to Matt, and he started laughing as he watched Bannister shove half of the sandwich into his mouth. Derrick was the star of the Alden hockey team and the catcher on the Alden baseball team. He was a good athlete, but since he played on the hockey team, he didn't go out for football.

"Hey, Bannister," Derrick said, laughing as Bannister shoved the rest of Matt's sandwich in his mouth. "Are you trying to starve the Panthers' new quarterback? They've got a game today, you know."

"I'm *not* the quarterback," Matt said sharply. "I'm the *running* back. I'm just substituting for Jesse until his ankle is better."

"Sorry," Derrick said, lifting his eyebrows.

Matt got the snap, then turned and pitched the ball to Russell. Russell put his head down and ran toward the sideline.

"Russell, cut through that hole!" Matt called out. "Cut!"

Russell didn't see the hole and kept running straight for the sideline. The St. Stephen's defense knocked Russell out of bounds at the Alden forty-one yard line—six yards short of the first down.

"Why wasn't *I* running the ball?" Matt muttered, as he kicked at the turf. He knew he would have seen the hole, cut toward the line of scrimmage, and dodged through the defense for a big gain. But he couldn't be too hard on Russell because he himself was having a hard time in his new position. He just wasn't getting the Panthers' offense in gear. The first quarter was almost over, and the Panthers were already down 7–0. St. Stephen's had the home field advantage, and they had scored on their first drive. Now it was third down and six, and the Panthers would have to pass.

"Forty-six, post pattern, on two," Matt said in the Panthers huddle. "Break!"

The play was easy. Josh was number forty-six, and he was supposed to run a post pattern. Matt would throw the pass to him before he turned around to look. If they were lucky, the Panthers would get a first down.

As Matt got set for the snap, he tried to remember whether he was supposed to count to four or five before he passed. His mind was a sudden blank, but there was no time to run over to Josh and ask him.

"Ready!" Matt shouted. "Hut, hut!"

Matt got the snap and faded back into the pocket. His offensive line was giving him good pass protection, and Matt had all the time he needed. He counted to four, and then threw the ball to Josh. The pass was a perfect spiral, sailing high through the blue sky—but it looked a little short.

Josh still hadn't turned around yet, and the pass defense had spotted the ball. When Josh did glance over his shoulder and saw that the pass was short, he tried to dive for it. A St. Stephen's safety cut in front of him and snagged the pass for an interception.

Matt felt his face get hot with anger, as he watched the St. Stephen's safety dodge through the Panthers players. The ball carrier broke through two tackles, then sprinted down the sideline toward the end zone.

Matt was the only person on the field who could stop him. He sprinted toward the St. Stephen's player, pumping his arms hard. The runner looked over and saw Matt closing in. He tried to cut around Matt, but Matt guessed what he was going to do, and leaped through the air.

Matt felt his shoulder pads smash against the runner's chest. The runner went flying, doing a half-flip and landing on his back out of bounds. Matt did a somersault and landed on his feet right by the Panthers bench.

"Nice tackle," Jesse said to him, slapping on the helmet. "Just forget about the interception. Get them next time."

Matt couldn't forget about the interception, though. St. Stephen's got the ball at the Alden twenty-eight-yard line. After three great passing plays, St. Stephen's put the ball across the goal line, to bring the score to St. Stephen's 14, Alden 0. They had turned the turnover into seven points.

The second half didn't go much better. Russell just wasn't as good a runner as Matt. The Panthers' ground game was getting nowhere.

At the beginning of the fourth quarter, Matt completed a few passes to Josh, advancing the Panthers to the St. Stephen's thirty-yard line. Matt was psyched. It was the first time the Panthers had been within striking distance of the end zone.

As soon as Matt released the ball on the next play, he knew the pass was perfect. Josh looked over his shoulder, keeping his eye on the ball until it fell right into his hands for a completion. Matt cheered as he watched Josh sprint all the way to the eight-yard-line—for a twenty-two-yard gain.

"Yes!" Matt cried, giving Josh a high five. "Great play!"

He had finally thrown a complete pass. It was almost as electrifying as making a great run. Now all the Panthers had to do was move the ball eight yards and they'd be back in the game.

The next play was a pitch-out to Dave, going to the right.

Matt got set for the snap, and looked over the defense. Suddenly his heart skipped a beat. He could tell that the defense had shifted to the right. If he didn't call an automatic, the play would be stopped at the line.

The cheering of the St. Stephen's crowd was loud, and Matt only had a split-second to think.

"Green 58," Matt shouted. "Hut, hut, hut!"

Matt received the snap. He spun around to give

the hand-off to Russell, but Russell and Dave were standing in the backfield, looking confused.

"Take the ball!" Matt shouted.

Russell started forward and turned for the ball. Matt tried to put the ball in Russell's stomach, but he hit Russell's elbow instead, and the ball bounced to the ground.

St. Stephen's recovered the fumble. Alden had blown its best chance to score. Matt kicked at the turf in frustration and walked over to the sidelines with his head down.

"What was that call you made out there?" Coach asked Matt. "There's no automatic called Green 58."

"Sorry, Coach," Matt said. "I guess I got confused."

Matt stood at the water cooler by himself. He knew that if Jesse were playing quarterback, the Panthers would be creaming St. Stephen's.

Instead, the Panthers ended up losing 14–0.

Matt was silent on the bus ride home. He felt like he had let the whole team down and he didn't want that to happen again.

He decided that if he had to be a quarterback, he was going to be a *good* quarterback.

"No," Matt muttered to himself, "a *great* quarterback!"

6

Matt grabbed the heaviest barbell from Jesse's set of weights, and tried to do a curl. He had always been strong. In gym class, he could always do more chin-ups than anyone else. Still, no matter how much he huffed and puffed and strained, Matt couldn't even lift the barbell above his waist.

"Look at Arnold Schwarzenneger," Josh said, laughing as he leaned against the wall in Jesse's basement. "He can't even do a little curl."

"Why don't *you* try lifting this barbell," Matt said, handing the barbell to Josh. Josh's arms were yanked straight down to the floor. The barbell crashed so loud that Mrs. Kissler called downstairs to see if everything was all right.

"Fine, Mom," Jesse called back, trying to keep from laughing at how stupid Josh had looked. "Matt and Josh are just helping me with my training."

"Well, try not to train so *loud*," Mrs. Kissler answered, closing the basement door.

It was a week after the St. Stephen's game, and the three friends were finishing up with the weights. Jesse had been working hard on his training, so that he could at least finish the season on the field. Matt could tell that Jesse's arms had gotten bigger and stronger.

"What did your doctor say this morning?" Matt asked Jesse.

"He said everything looked great," Jesse answered. "I might be able to come back sooner than I thought."

"When does your cast come off?" Josh asked.

"Not for another four weeks. Then it will be another two weeks until I can get back out on the field, even for practice."

"That's more than a *month* from now," Matt said, pulling his Alden sweat shirt over his head. "I guess that means I'll be the quarterback for the Williamsport game."

"I really wish I could play in that game," Jesse said, wiping his brow with a towel. "I want to show that jerk Anderson a thing or two."

"Don't worry, Jesse," Matt said, tossing a football up and down. "I'll be ready for Anderson. From now on I'm going to work on being a good quarterback."

"You're not going to steal my position, are you?" Jesse joked, knocking on his cast. "I won't have this stupid plaster on forever, you know."

"I'm just trying to help the team," Matt said.

"Then you'd better work on your passing," Jesse said. "Let's go outside, and I'll teach you everything I know."

Jesse's backyard was big. In the summer, whenever the fields at the park were taken, Jesse and his friends played baseball games there. The yard was lined with tall trees, and the grass was thick and green. It was a perfect place to practice passing, too, and the three friends got right to work.

Jesse handed his crutches to Matt, and got ready to throw the first pass.

"Go deep for a bomb, flag pattern, on three," Jesse told Josh. "Ready! Hut, hut, hut."

Josh ran forward at half-speed. After ten paces, he broke right and sprinted toward the oak tree at top speed. Jesse stepped forward and cranked the ball before Josh had even looked. Matt was amazed at the pass. Josh didn't have to break his stride. All he did was glance over his shoulder, lift up his arms, and let the ball fall into his hands.

"Incredible!" Matt said, slapping Jesse a high five. "I can't believe you can throw the ball that far wearing a cast."

"That's why I've been working with the weights," Jesse answered, as Josh jogged back with the ball. "When I get back to playing quarterback, I'm going to be stronger than ever."

"Your turn, Matt," Josh said, tossing him the ball. "I'll run the exact same pattern. Remember, on the bomb, flag pattern, I count to eight. You throw the ball on six."

"Got it," Matt said. "Hut, hut, hut."

Josh ran forward, then sprinted toward the oak tree. When Matt had counted to six, he cranked the ball into the air.

The pass wobbled like a wounded bird, flipping end

over end. When Josh finally glanced over his shoulder, the pass had already fallen to the grass fifteen yards short.

"You're trying to throw too hard," Jesse said. "Just pretend you're throwing a baseball to first base. It's the exact same motion."

"Okay," Matt said, concentrating. "I'll just throw it nice and easy."

"This time, I'll run a hook pattern, on two," Josh said, tossing the ball back to Matt. "This one takes good timing. When I turn around and face you, the ball had better be there. If not, we give the defense time to get in place."

"Right," Matt said "Hut, hut!"

Josh sprinted full speed from the line of scrimmage. Matt threw the ball just as Josh was turning around for the hook. It was good timing, but the throw was too high. Josh jumped, but he couldn't get a hand on it.

After two hours, however, the hard work started paying off. Matt began to get the feel of passing the football. Now he knew what Jesse meant about not throwing the ball too hard. It didn't mean that he was supposed to throw the ball softly—he was just supposed to let his arm do the work. He threw more and more spirals, and Josh was catching more and more of his passes.

"I've had enough," Josh said at last, walking back after another pass pattern. "I think I've run about twenty miles this afternoon."

"I've got an idea," Matt said, with a sly smile. "Let's race to Pete's. The first person there gets to order anything from the menu. Okay?"

"How about the *last* person there?" Josh said, sitting down on the ground to rest. "Hey, maybe you guys should *carry* me to Pete's?"

The three friends ended up asking Mrs. Kissler to drive them to the Cranbrook Mall, because it was too far for Jesse to walk there with crutches. They ordered a pizza, then settled into their favorite booth. Before they could even take their first bites, the door swung open and a group of boys strolled in wearing Williamsport jackets.

Anderson was leading the pack.

Matt dropped his slice of pizza and felt his face get hot with anger. Jesse dropped his pizza, too, then pushed himself up on his crutches and faced Anderson. Anderson had blond hair and huge arms. His neck seemed as thick as a garbage can, and he stood three inches taller then Jesse.

"Oh, it's the poor injured quarterback," Anderson said to Jesse, smiling. The boys behind him laughed, as if Anderson had just said the funniest thing in the world.

Matt and Josh rose from the booth and stood beside Jesse.

"I ought to punch you in the face," Jesse said. "You gave me a late hit, and broke my ankle."

"Gee, I'm sorry," Anderson said. He stepped closer to Matt. "And guess what? When we play you guys next, I'm going to smash your *new* quarterback, too."

"You're a total loser," Matt answered, pushing Anderson in the chest. "Why don't you lay off?"

The smile vanished from Anderson's face and his buddies stopped laughing. Pete's Pizza got very quiet.

"You shouldn't have done that," Anderson said, giving Matt a huge push. Matt went flying back against a booth, then fell to the floor. When he got to his feet, Matt was so mad that he was ready to take on the whole Williamsport gang by himself. Josh and Jesse held him back.

"You just wait until we meet on the field!" Matt said, pointing to Anderson.

Anderson laughed. "We beat you once, and we'll beat you again."

"We'll see about that," Matt answered, but Anderson had already turned around and headed for the door. The Williamsport gang followed right behind.

The three friends sat down and looked at their pizza, but they were all too angry to eat a bite.

"When do we play Williamsport?" Josh asked.

"In four weeks," Matt answered, still fuming. "And I plan to be ready."

7

It was the best drive of the game, and Matt was totally pumped up. The Panthers had started on their own thirty-nine-yard line, and now they were working from a first down on the Lincoln twenty-eight. Matt wanted to put some points on the board before the whistle sounded for halftime.

The score was Lincoln 7, Alden 0. There were only fifty-eight seconds left on the time clock, and the Panthers would have to work fast.

"Okay, remember to run the ball out of bounds,"

Matt said in the huddle. He intended to stop the clock, and give his team more time. "Got it? Hand-off, thirty-eight, on two. Break!"

The Panthers jogged to the line of scrimmage and crouched down. The Lincoln defense lined up against them, and Matt got in position for the snap.

"Ready!" Matt called, "Hut, hut!"

Matt felt the ball snap into his hands. He turned to his left and fixed his eyes on Russell's far hip. Russell rushed forward, holding his arms for the hand-off, and Matt placed the ball gently on target. Russell snatched the ball away, broke left, and headed for the sideline.

Matt watched as Russell crossed the line of scrimmage and rushed toward a group of defensemen. He hoped Russell would be able to get out of bounds, and stop the clock. But Russell was in trouble with the Lincoln defense.

"Cut left!" Matt cried out, but Russell was tackled on the twenty-four-yard line, for a gain of four yards.

The clock was still ticking—forty-five seconds, forty-four, forty-three . . .

The Panthers ran back as fast as they could and got into the huddle. Coach didn't have time to call in a play, so Matt was on his own. He had to think fast.

"QB option, on three," Matt said. "Break!"

Matt checked the clock as he jogged to the line of scrimmage—thirty-one seconds left. Russell had wasted fifteen seconds by not getting out of bounds. Matt knew that he *had* to get out of bounds, even if it meant not getting a first down.

He got the snap and faded to his left, running toward the sideline. Russell was running just behind him, ready to get the pitch-out. Matt checked out the Lincoln safety. He could tell the safety was expecting the pitch-out, because he was keying on Russell. That was just what Matt wanted. It meant he got to run the ball.

Matt cut sharply across the line of scrimmage, scooting right around the Lincoln safety. The linebackers were after him, and he knew he should head for the sideline and run out of bounds.

But it felt so good to be running that he decided to take a chance. He saw a hole between the two linebackers, gave a head fake, then dodged between them for a first down. It looked like the gamble had paid off. There was an open field between him and the goal line.

Then he felt a hand grab his ankle, and he fell in a heap on the sixteen-yard line. One of the linebackers had sneaked up behind him for a shoestring tackle.

Matt jumped up from the ground swearing at himself. He had screwed up by not getting the ball out of bounds, and the clock was still ticking—twenty-three seconds, twenty-two, twenty-one . . .

Only an amazing play would be able to put the Panthers on the board before halftime. Matt knew that he couldn't let the pressure get to him, or he'd make a mistake.

"Forty-six, flag pattern, on three!" he yelled in the huddle. "Break."

The Panthers got to the line of scrimmage with twelve seconds left on the clock. Matt got the snap and faded back into the pocket.

The Lincoln defense was blitzing, and the linebackers broke through the Panthers' line. Matt scrambled out of the way of the linebackers, ducking under one tackle and spinning off another. He looked for Josh upfield, but the pass defense was strong. He looked for his secondary receivers but they were all covered, too.

Looking again to Josh, he saw that Josh had pulled ahead of the defenders. Matt knew he didn't have much time to get the pass off, because Josh was running right for the sideline. So he whipped the ball as hard as he could, and hoped that his arm was good enough.

Josh jumped up, grabbed the ball in midair, and landed with both feet *just* inside the end zone. He tumbled with the ball out of bounds just as the whistle sounded.

The Panthers bench went crazy. Matt's pass had been perfect, and the Panthers had put six points on the board. Matt ran off the field slapping high fives to everyone.

Matt watched the extra-point attempt from the sideline. Duke was the kicker and Russell was the holder. Russell got the snap from Bruce, but he bobbled it. As Duke stepped forward, Russell managed to get control of the ball. He spun the laces toward the goal right as Duke swung his foot. The kick veered to the left and bounced off the upright. The Panthers jogged to the locker room down by one point.

"Nice pass out there," Jesse said in the locker room at halftime. "I guess all of our practice really paid off."

"It sure did," Matt said with a smile. "I'm even starting to like playing quarterback."

"Good," Coach Litzinger said, overhearing them.

"Now listen up, everyone." He knocked on a locker to get the team's attention. "Lincoln is a weak team. We should be tearing them apart. Let's get back out there and concentrate on getting first downs. Don't worry about the big touchdown play. Just keep getting first downs, and pretty soon you'll get the ball across the end zone. Now let's get out there and show Lincoln what the Alden Panthers are all about!"

The team let out a yell and charged toward the locker room door, but Coach held Matt back.

"You're doing a nice job out there, Matt," Coach said. "Just remember to keep your cool and stay alert."

Matt nodded and jogged out to the field. Part of him wanted to run the ball—and score the big touchdowns—but part of him now also enjoyed passing the ball, and calling automatics, and throwing pitchouts, and scrambling.

Being a quarterback was like being the captain of a ship. The truth was, Matt wasn't exactly looking forward to Jesse taking over as quarterback again.

Most of the second half was a battle of the defense. The Alden defense was strong, and Lincoln wasn't able to put any more points on the board. The Panthers had a few chances to score, but Russell and

Dave didn't come through with the big runs. With only a minute and twenty-one seconds left in the game, the score was still Lincoln 7, Alden 6.

The Panthers had just returned a punt to Lincoln's thirty-four-yard line. Matt knew he had to score on this drive, or the game would be lost.

The first play was a pitch-out to Russell, who was tackled on the line of scrimmage. On the next play, Coach called for a flag pattern pass to Josh. Matt's heart was pounding as he got ready for the snap.

"Hut, hut, hut!"

The pass protection was good and Matt had all the time he needed. He looked upfield and saw that Josh had beaten his defender, and was wide open. If he could only get the ball to Josh, the Panthers would probably score, and win the game.

Matt cocked his arm and fired. The throw was too far in front. Josh dived for it, but missed it by a foot. Matt knew that his bad pass might cost the Panthers the game.

Now it was third down and ten. The next call was for a post-pattern pass to Duke. They needed a first down, or the game would be all but over. There were only forty-nine seconds left on the clock.

Matt got the snap and faded back. Duke was covered like a rug, and there was no way Matt could get the pass to him. So he checked his secondary receiver, but Josh was tightly covered as well. Matt didn't know what to do. He had no receivers open, and the defense was closing in.

He had to run for it. Tucking the ball under his arm, Matt dodged around the charging linebacker. He crossed the line of scrimmage, broke free of a tackle, and started sprinting down the sideline. The free safety rushed over to knock him out of bounds, but Matt changed direction and cut around him. He headed across the field toward the opposite side of the end zone, leaving the other cornerbacks in the dust.

Matt grinned as he crossed the end zone for a touchdown. He spiked the ball and did his stutter-step dance. A few seconds later he was mobbed by the Panthers team. It had been an incredible thirty-five-yard run, and the Panthers had just won the game, 12–7.

Jesse came up to Matt in the locker room and slapped him a high five. Matt looked down at Jesse's cast and saw his big red signature, MATT GREENE— RUNNING BACK.

"I guess I did okay as *quarterback* today," Matt said proudly.

"You made some mistakes," Jesse said. "But we

can work on those. Besides, your big play was a *running* play."

"I might have looked like a running back," Matt said, standing up to leave. "But I was a *quarterback*."

"Oh," Jesse said. "I thought *I* was still the Panthers' quarterback."

Matt didn't answer—he was already gone.

8

"If you don't quit arguing, we won't have time to play at all," Duke said impatiently, as he picked up the football from the ground. "We've been standing here for ten minutes, while you two try to figure out who's going to play quarterback."

"Relax, Duke," Matt said, patting him on the back. "We'll have time to play."

It was lunch, and the boys were getting ready to play a game of two-hand touch in back of the school. Matt and Russell both wanted to play quarterback.

Jesse was leaning up against his crutches, listening to the argument.

"Every day at lunch, you get to play quarterback," Matt said to Russell. "I just think it's my turn."

"But you get to play quarterback on the *real* team," Russell answered. "So it's fair."

"I say it's my turn," Matt said.

"*I'll* play quarterback!" Bannister said at last, grabbing the ball away from Duke. "Go long, Duke," Bannister said with a smile. "Go out for the bomb!"

Duke took off running and Bannister faded back, his big belly bouncing up and down. Everyone laughed as Bannister waved Duke farther and farther down the field, until Duke was all the way at the other end.

Bannister finally took his arm back and heaved a throw. The ball wobbled end over end, and landed about twenty feet away. Everyone clapped and whistled, while Bannister took a bow.

"Now I know why you like being quarterback so much, Matt," Bannister said, smiling. "It's the greatest position, just like you said."

"Hey, Matt," Jesse said, hopping over toward Matt on his crutches. "Did you really tell Bannister that quarterback was the greatest position?"

"Well . . ." Matt said, feeling a little embarrassed. "I guess it's better than I thought it would be."

"Oh, really?" Jesse said impatiently. "You mean you'd rather be a quarterback than a running back?"

"I don't know," Matt answered with a shrug.

"It sounds like Matt is trying to steal your position," Bannister said, nudging Jesse and giving him a wink. Bannister liked to stir up trouble. It was his idea of fun.

"That *is* what it sounds like," Jesse said, staring angrily at Matt. "I never should have helped you with your passing. Now you think you're the greatest quarterback since Joe Montana."

"Hey . . ." Matt began.

"Just remember something," Jesse interrupted angrily. "I get my cast off in two weeks, and I'm going to be back on the field pretty soon. Then we'll see who the best quarterback is!"

"I guess we will," Matt answered, getting angry himself.

"You'll never be able to pass the ball like me," Jesse said, turning around to walk away. "No matter how hard you try."

"Oh, yeah?" Matt answered. "I guess we'll just let Coach decide. By the way, after yesterday's game,

Coach told me I was doing a great job at quarter-back."

"Oh, yeah?" Jesse answered. "If *I* had been playing quarterback yesterday, we would have beaten Lincoln by at least thirty points. Instead, we just barely won."

Bannister stepped between them and held up his arms.

"The judges have ruled that this boxing match is a tie," Bannister said. He tried to grab the two friends' arms and lift them up in victory, but Matt yanked his arm away.

"You're not very funny, Bannister," Matt said, turning to leave.

After practice that afternoon, Matt and Josh went to Matt's house to practice passing. Matt's backyard wasn't as big as Jesse's, but it would have to do. Since their argument at lunch, Matt didn't really feel like hanging out at Jesse's house.

Josh went deep for a bomb, and Matt dropped back to pass. Just as Matt was bringing his arm around to throw, he heard a big "Boo!" behind him. He jerked his arm down and the pass went straight into the ground.

Matt whipped around and saw his father standing behind him.

"Dad, I was trying to pass," Matt said.

"I know," Mr. Greene answered. "I just wanted to see how hard you were concentrating."

"I guess not hard enough," Matt said.

"Don't worry," Mr. Greene answered. "If you had snuck up on *me,* I probably would have jumped out of my skin, too."

"Hey, Mr. Greene," Josh said, throwing the football from across the yard. "Catch!"

Big Bill Greene dropped his jacket on the ground, and ran under the ball. Then he bent down and caught the ball behind his back, with one hand.

"Awesome catch," Josh said, running up. "Do you want to play with us, Mr. Greene?".

"Well . . ." Mr. Greene said, clearing his throat. "I'm not in the shape I used to be. I think you kids would leave me in the dust."

"Oh, come on, Dad," Matt said. "Just throw the ball with us for a little while."

"Well, okay," Mr. Greene said, gripping his big hand around the football. "Here's the play. Matt, you're defense. Josh, you're offense. I want you to run to the maple tree in the Jensons' yard, then look for the bomb. Just watch out for Mrs. Jenson's flowers."

"All the way to the maple tree in the Jensons' yard?" Josh said, amazed. "Can you really throw the ball that far?"

"Let's find out," Mr. Greene said. "Ready! Hut, hut!"

Josh took off across the grass, under an apple tree, over a flower garden, and around some bushes. Matt was right behind him the whole way. After it seemed like they had run forever, they approached the maple tree and Josh turned around for the pass.

"Wow!" both friends shouted, as they watched the football come sailing over the apple tree, over the garden and the bushes, then hit the top branches of the maple tree with a crash. They both ran under the tree, to wait for the ball to come down—but it didn't.

"Who caught the pass?" Mr. Greene shouted across the yard.

"The maple tree!" Matt called back.

"Uh-oh," Mr. Greene answered. "Well, somebody better climb up and get it."

Josh scrambled up the tree in a flash, climbing hand over hand. He snatched the ball from the branches, then dropped it right into Matt's arms.

"Interception!" Matt shouted, joking. "It never touched the ground!"

"You wish," Josh answered, dropping from the branches.

They ran back into Matt's backyard but Mr. Greene had already put his jacket back on.

"That's enough football for me," Mr. Greene said, heading for the house. "I'm getting too old to throw bombs."

"I wish *I* could throw like that," Josh said.

"Me too," Matt answered.

"Then just keep practicing!" Mr. Greene said, as he vanished into the house.

9

Matt and Jesse always sat next to each other in English class. Usually their teacher, Mrs. Chapman, had to yell at them to stop talking and passing notes. That week, however, Matt and Jesse had hardly said a word to each other, and for the first time the back of the classroom was quiet.

On the day of the North Colby game, Jesse came late to class. He stretched his cast out into the aisle as he sat down in his chair. Matt looked at it. The first thing he noticed was that his big signature—

MATT GREENE, RUNNING BACK—had been crossed out with a black marker.

"Why'd you cross out my name?" Matt asked, whispering so Mrs. Chapman wouldn't hear.

"You know why," Jesse answered quietly. "Because you're trying to steal my position."

"Did you ever think that I might be a better quarterback than you?" Matt asked, feeling his face get hot. "Huh?"

"In your dreams," Jesse said, without even looking over.

"You just watch me at the game against North Colby today," Matt whispered. "You'll see."

"North Colby is the worst team in the conference," Jesse answered. "You'd *better* beat them—and by about thirty points."

"Enough back there!" Mrs. Chapman said at last. "I was hoping that you two would be quiet for the rest of the year!"

"Okay, men," Coach said to the team, just before kick-off that afternoon. It was a cool day, and the leaves were turning orange and yellow around the North Colby football field. "Everybody knows that North Colby is in last place, and that they haven't won a single game all season. But don't let that fool you. We've got to go out there and play our hardest, just as if we were playing for the championship. And remember, we play Williamsport next week, and we don't want to get sloppy. Okay? Now let's play ball!"

The Panthers' defense was one of the best in the conference, and the weak North Colby offense couldn't gain any yardage. North Colby only made three first downs in the whole first half. They never even made it into the Panthers' territory.

An equally weak North Colby defense made it possible for Matt to have a fairly easy time at quarterback.

"Pitch-out, thirty-eight left, on three," Matt said in the huddle, toward the end of the first half. The Panthers had already scored a touchdown—on a great run by Dave McShea—and the score was Alden 7, North Colby 0. Now they were on the North Colby thirty-eight-yard line, working from a first down.

Matt got ready for the snap, and looked over the defensive lineup. North Colby had set up strong on the left, just where Russell was supposed to run with the pitch-out. Matt knew he should call an automatic—the hand-off to the right—and this time he knew he'd call the correct numbers.

"Green 18," Matt shouted in a confident voice. "Hut, hut, hut!"

Matt turned to his right, and saw Dave rush toward him for the hand-off. Matt placed the ball gently into Dave's arms, and Dave broke to the right, while Russell blocked. The North Colby defense was out of position for a play to the right, and Dave had a huge empty field. He sprinted all the way down to the North Colby twenty-two before he was tackled.

"Good call!" Russell told Matt as they got into the huddle.

The next play was a post-pattern pass to Duke. Matt got the snap, faded back, and waited for Duke to break toward the goal post. Duke was being covered tightly by a defender, and Matt didn't know if he should throw or not. The last thing he wanted to do was throw an interception. At the last second he decided to pass, and brought his arm back. Just as he was bringing his arm around, he saw that Josh was wide open on the sideline, and tried to stop his throw. The ball slipped out of his hand.

Matt's heart dropped as he watched the ball flutter in the air, end over end. A North Colby lineman jumped for it, but Bruce, the Panthers' center, leaped in front of him and caught the ball. Bruce landed on the ground, and was mobbed by three North Colby players.

The referee dropped his flag and blew his whistle.

"Ineligible pass receiver upfield," the referee said, gesturing to the scorekeeper. "Five-yard penalty."

Now the Panthers were back on the thirty-three-yard line, and it was second down. Coach called for another pass play—a short screen to Russell, on three.

"Hut, hut, hut!"

Matt faded back for the pass, hoping that he could finally make a completion. Matt wanted to move the Panthers upfield, but he also wanted to show Jesse that he could pass the ball.

Russell crossed the line of scrimmage, and Matt put the ball into the air. Just when Russell turned around for the catch, a North Colby safety jumped and made a beautiful interception. Matt was so surprised that he just stood there for a second, watching the North Colby player run with the ball toward the Alden end zone.

Matt couldn't believe he had just given up an interception.

Russell finally grabbed hold of the ball-carrier and slammed him to the ground. As Matt was running over to help, he saw the ball jar loose and roll across the grass. He snatched up the fumble and took off.

Sprinting through the North Colby defense, Matt

dodged and cut and jumped, leaving North Colby players sprawled out behind him. Finally he crossed the goal line, spiked the ball, and did his victory dance.

Matt was psyched, and the Panthers went into halftime with a lead of 14–0.

"You're not making many pass completions out there," Jesse said to Matt, as the team headed to the locker room.

"Hey, we're ahead by fourteen points, aren't we?" Matt said. "I don't think that's so bad."

"But what if that North Colby guy hadn't fumbled?" Jesse said. "Then what?"

Matt didn't feel like listening to Jesse. He wanted to complete passes, but he figured a quarterback's job was to put points on the board, and any way they got the points was fine.

It was third down and ten, and Matt faded back for a long pass to Josh. He had only thrown two complete passes in the whole second half. Now that the game was almost over, he really wanted to nail this throw.

Josh was open, and Matt hurled the pass. As soon as he let it go, he knew the pass was perfect. Josh jumped up to catch it, but the ball bounced off his shoulder pad and fell to the ground. Matt clapped his hands in frustration.

"Sorry about that," Josh said, as they walked back to the huddle. "I should have caught it."

"It's okay," Matt said. "We're still ahead by four-teen."

Since it was fourth down, and the Panthers were on the twenty-three-yard line, they decided to kick for a field goal.

Russell knelt on the grass, and caught the snap from Bruce. He quickly put one end of the ball on the grass, holding the other end with his finger. Duke ran up and kicked the ball, soccer-style, right through the goal-posts for a field goal.

Those were the last points the Panthers scored, and they won the game 17–0.

"You're going to have to play better than that to beat Williamsport next week," Jesse said to Matt on the bus ride home.

"Don't worry about it," Matt answered, trying to sound confident. "Williamsport will be no problem."

10

"What's everybody doing over there?" Matt asked Bannister, pointing toward a big group of football players. The two of them were sitting in the cafeteria, their lunches spread before them. "It looks like a huge huddle."

"It's Jesse," Bannister said, popping his last cheese curl into his mouth. "He just got back from the doctor. They finally took his cast off."

"Oh," Matt said quietly. "That's great."

It was the day of the big Williamsport game, and

again Matt was too nervous to eat. All morning long, he had been thinking about Anderson, and the powerful Williamsport defense. He wanted to beat Williamsport more than anything. That way, he could get back at Anderson for pushing him down at Pete's Pizza—and he could also show Jesse that he was a good quarterback.

Matt glanced up and saw Jesse coming across the cafeteria toward him. Although Jesse was still on crutches, it was the first time in six weeks he was wearing both shoes.

"I got my cast off this morning," Jesse began, pulling his chair up to the table. "The doctor says I'll be back on the field in two weeks. I'm going to work hard to get back in shape."

"Good," Matt answered, half-heartedly.

"Hey, Jesse," Bannister said, with his mouth full of food. "Don't you think Matt should have something to eat? He's got to play in the big Williamsport game today."

"Speaking of the Williamsport game," Jesse said to Matt. "Anderson is the guy who fractured my ankle, and I really want us to win."

"So do I," Matt answered.

"I have some advice," Jesse said. "The only way we can beat Williamsport is to pass the ball. Anderson can stop our ground game, especially since you're not at running back."

"Thanks for the advice," Matt said grumpily.

"I sure wish *I* could be out there today," Jesse said as he stood up to walk away. "And in a few weeks, I *will* be."

"Okay, men," Coach Litzinger said, as the team huddled around him on the sideline. "This is a big game. Williamsport is our biggest competitor for the championship. Forget about our preseason scrimmage. This game is all that matters now. Let's do it, Panthers!"

The whole team cheered. As the offense ran onto the field for the kick-off, Coach pulled Matt aside.

"Just remember what we talked about in the locker room," Coach said. "I'll be calling a lot of pass plays. It's the only way we can beat these guys. Keep your cool and give it your best. Take the game one play at a time."

"Sure, Coach," Matt answered, turning to run onto the field.

Matt got back deep for the kick-off return. He looked ahead at the Williamsport defense. When he saw Anderson, Matt's heart skipped a beat. Anderson looked bigger than ever in his football gear. Matt took a deep breath, and then the referee blew his whistle for the kick.

The kick was low, just the way Matt liked it. He snagged the ball, tucked it into his side, and got a good jump on the run. The Panthers blocking spread out in front of him, trying to knock a hole in the Williamsport defense. Matt followed Bruce Judge past the twenty-five-yard line, then darted left into the center of the field. Out of the corner of his eye, Matt saw three defensemen barreling toward him, and changed direction.

He was running at full speed again, when he felt his legs get cut out from beneath him. He did a full cartwheel in midair, then crumpled to the ground in a heap. He saw stars for a second, and when his eyes cleared Anderson was standing right above him.

"Hi, quarterback," Anderson said, in a teasing voice. "I hope I didn't hurt you."

"Get lost," Matt said, standing up. He was still a little dizzy, and almost fell back down.

"Feeling sick?" Anderson asked.

"You're real funny," Matt answered.

He walked back to the huddle. Coach was calling for a hand-off to Russell. Matt hoped that Russell was going to have a good day. If Russell gained some yardage, Matt wouldn't have to throw so much.

"Hut, hut!"

Matt got the snap, turned around, and handed the ball to Russell. Russell tried to run it straight up the middle, but Anderson jumped through the defense and knocked Russell to the ground, for a loss of a yard. Matt knew Coach would call a pass next, and he was right.

"Hook pattern, forty-three, on two," Matt said in the huddle. "Break."

Matt faded back into the pocket, looking for Josh to break and turn around for the hook. The Alden offensive line was holding back Williamsport pretty well. Then Anderson knocked Bruce to the ground and came charging at Matt full speed. Matt tried to duck to the side of Anderson, but Anderson stuck out his arm and grabbed him by the front of his jersey. Matt tried to spin away, but Anderson had already gotten his other hand on Matt's shoulder. He yanked Matt to the ground, and then fell on top of him.

"What's wrong?" Anderson said, as he let go of Matt and got up. "The Panthers don't look so hot today."

Matt was too mad to answer. The Panthers had lost six yards on their first two plays, and that wasn't a good sign. Matt got right back in the huddle. Coach called for a long pass—a flag pattern, to Josh, on three.

"Hut, hut, hut!"

Josh beat his pass defenders with a head fake, then sprinted out into the open for the pass. Matt saw that Josh was wide open, and began to count in his head. He took his arm back and chucked the ball. Josh dove for the pass, but it was too far out in front. It was fourth down and sixteen yards, and the Panthers had to punt.

It had been a bad first possession for Alden, and it turned out to be a great first possession for Williamsport. They received the punt, ran it back into Alden territory, and then put the ball over the goal line in four plays.

"I don't believe it," Matt said, tossing his water cup to the ground as he watched the action from the sidelines.

It was going to be a very tough game.

Anderson and the Williamsport defense shut out the Panthers in the first half. After the first Williamsport touchdown, however, the Panthers only allowed Williamsport a field goal. So when the teams ran back onto the field for the second half, the score was Williamsport 10, Alden 0.

Matt knew he had to get his passing game into gear. There was no way that Russell and Dave could gain enough yards on the ground to get first downs.

"Hut, hut, hut!" Matt shouted. He got the snap, but the ball felt strange. The laces weren't across his fingers. As he ran back for the hand-off, Matt tried to get the correct grip. He looked down at the ball and lost sight of the target for the hand-off—Russell's far hip. Matt put the hand-off right into Russell's side, and the ball fell to the ground.

Luckily, Dave was there to drop on the fumble. Matt was mad at himself, but he also knew that *he* would have been able to hold onto the hand-off if *he* were the running back.

It was third down and nine, and the Panthers were on their own forty-two-yard line. The call was for a play-action pass to Josh.

This time, Matt positioned his hands correctly for the snap. He got the ball with the laces across his fingers, and turned around for the fake hand-off. With both hands on the ball, Matt stuck it into Dave's stomach, and then pulled it out with one hand. He turned to watch Dave run, hiding the ball to his side, so that the defense would think Dave had the ball.

He saw Josh speeding across in front of him, wide

open, and threw the ball. It was a clothes-line pass, fast and low and straight.

It was a little *too* low. Anderson dove to the side and got a hand on the ball. Matt held his breath as he watched the ball flip up into the air. Players from both teams scrambled for it. The referee blew his whistle to end the play, but Matt couldn't tell which side had caught the ball. Finally the ref pointed to the Williamsport goal, and the Williamsport fans went crazy.

Anderson looked over and pointed his finger at Matt. "Looks like you blew another play, hotshot," he said.

Matt walked off the field. He didn't feel like talking to anyone. He wished the game were already over. It seemed that no matter how hard he tried, he couldn't move the ball for the Panthers. So it was no surprise to him when the Panthers ended up losing the game 21–0.

11

When Matt walked into English class the next morning, he couldn't wait to talk with Jesse. He put his books down on the desk and swung into his seat. Jesse didn't look over.

"Hi, Jesse," Matt said.

Jesse just nodded.

"How's your ankle feeling?" Matt asked.

"Okay," Jesse answered.

"I hope you'll be ready to play in the South Colby game next week," Matt said.

Jesse finally looked at his friend. "I thought *you* wanted to be the quarterback," he said.

"No way," Matt said, smiling. "Quarterbacking is boring."

"But I thought you liked quarterback! I thought you said it was the coolest position on the team."

"Are you kidding?" Matt said. "Running back has all the glory. You get to run and dodge and spin out of tackles. Plus you get to score all the touchdowns. All the quarterback does is pass. Totally boring."

Jesse broke into a big smile.

"You're crazy," Jesse answered. "The quarterback controls all the action."

It felt just like old times again.

"Well *you* can be quarterback if you want to," Matt said, putting his hand out for Jesse to slap. "I think *I'd* rather be a running back."

Jesse laughed and slapped Matt's hand.

"You've got a deal," Jesse said. "But what made you change your mind?"

"The Williamsport game," Matt answered. "I'll never be able to throw the ball like you. You've got the best arm in the conference."

"And Russell will never be able to run like *you*,"

Jesse said. "The Panthers really need you in the backfield."

"When does the doctor say you can play again?" Matt asked.

"He says two weeks. But I think I can come back sooner."

"You have to," said Matt. "We need you for the South Colby game next week. If we lose that game, we don't have any chance of making it to the championships."

Jesse nodded. "I know. But if I'm going to be ready to play next week, I'll need your help."

"You've got it," Matt said.

"Boys! Be quiet!" Mrs. Chapman said, trying to begin the class.

Matt and Jesse looked at each other and smiled. Everything was back to normal.

Before practice that afternoon, Coach Litzinger pulled Matt and Jesse aside. The two friends were sitting on a bench in the locker room, wearing their white practice uniforms. Coach Litzinger was leaning against the lockers, holding a bag of footballs.

"It's good to see you ready for action again, Jesse,"

Coach said. "But it may take some time for you to get back into top shape. I know you want to play quarterback soon, but Matt has been doing a nice job. We'll just have to wait and see how things work out."

Matt cleared his throat. "Uh, Coach?" Matt began. "I really think Jesse should be the quarterback against South Colby. We need his arm to win."

"And we need Matt's running, too," Jesse added.

"Well . . ." Coach said, rubbing his chin. "What does your doctor say, Jesse?"

"He says I'll definitely be ready to play next week," Jesse said.

Matt's face turned red. Jesse's doctor had said it would be at least *two* weeks before Jesse could play. Matt didn't say anything, though. The Panthers needed Jesse back as soon as possible.

"That sounds good to me," Coach said, leading the boys toward the field. "But don't work yourself too hard. Your legs are going to be weak, and so's your ankle."

Coach said it was alright for Jesse to run a few plays. He wanted Jesse to get back into action, but he worried that his star quarterback might hurt himself again.

When practice started, the Panthers were psyched to have Jesse back in the huddle. And Matt was psyched to be a running back again.

"Hut, hut!" Jesse cried.

Matt rushed forward from the backfield, and lifted his arms for the hand-off. Jesse placed the ball on Matt's hip, and Matt closed his arms around it. As he bounded forward, Matt scanned the defense for holes. Just then the offensive line bashed open a hole, and Matt cut through it, twisting his body as he ran. After gaining five more yards, he was brought down by Chip Simon, the middle line-backer.

On the next play, Jesse faded back for a short screen pass to Matt. Matt rushed across the line of scrimmage and turned around just as Jesse released the ball. The pass was a perfect spiral, and as fast as a bullet. Matt snatched the ball, then broke right and charged up the sideline.

He had almost forgotten how much fun it was to run.

Matt glanced over his shoulder and saw Chip chasing after him. It didn't look like Matt could go any faster, but somehow he shifted into a higher gear and sped ahead, leaving Chip in the dust. A second later, he crossed the goal line.

"Nice throw!" Matt said to Jesse, back in the huddle.

"Nice *run*," Jesse answered, slapping Matt's hand.

12

On the day of the South Colby game, Matt, Jesse, and Josh were eating lunch in the cafeteria when Bannister and Derrick walked up to their table. Derrick sat down, but Bannister stood right behind Matt.

"What are you doing back there?" Matt asked, as he turned around to see what Bannister was up to.

"You guys have a game today, don't you?" Bannister answered, eyeing Matt's sandwich. "You never eat on a game day."

"Oh, I get it," Matt said, taking a huge bite of his sandwich. "You hope I'm too nervous to eat again."

"Why don't you ask your mom to pack more stuff in your lunch bag?" Josh asked Bannister. "That way you wouldn't have to beg."

"I'm supposed to be on a diet," Bannister said, blushing. "All she gives me is an apple and some celery."

"An apple and some celery?" Matt said, starting to laugh. "No wonder you're always begging for other people's food."

"We don't want Bannister to lose too much weight, though," Derrick said. "Hockey season is coming up soon, and Bannister is our special pond tester."

"Pond tester?" Matt asked. "What's that?"

"When we want to test the ice on Black's Pond to see if it's thick enough," Derrick explained, smiling, "we send Bannister out first. If the ice can hold *him* up, then we know it can hold anybody."

"That's right!" Bannister said, reaching in for Matt's potato chips. "It's a matter of safety. You'd better give me your chips *and* your cookies."

Matt slapped Bannister's hand away. "Forget it," he said, laughing. "Besides, I'm starving. I'm not nervous anymore, now that I'm running back again. In fact, I can't wait for the game this afternoon."

Matt ripped open his chips and started stuffing them into his mouth.

"Here you go, Bannister," Jesse said, handing Bannister his uneaten sandwich. "I guess *I'm* the nervous one today."

"Why?" Bannister asked as he took a bite.

"I haven't played in a real game all season," Jesse answered. "And I just hope my ankle is strong enough. The doctor said I wasn't really supposed to play for another week, so I'm not going to be able to scramble very well."

"You're not a speed-demon anyway," Bannister said. "In fact, I bet *I* could beat you in a race."

"That's all I need to hear," Jesse said.

That afternoon, time was running out in the first half, and the Panthers were behind by a score of 7–0.

On second down, Matt burst from the backfield and opened up his arms for the fake hand-off. Jesse faded back, put the ball in Matt's stomach, and then pulled it out. Matt rushed into the South Colby defense, dodging and faking like he really had the ball. Finally a South Colby guard rammed into him and brought him down. Matt crashed to the ground, then looked up to see how Jesse was doing with the pass.

Jesse was in trouble. The defense had broken through the line, and a South Colby tackle was chasing after him in the backfield.

Jesse tried to run around the tackle, ducking his head and sprinting to the side. The trouble was, Jesse just wasn't fast enough. The tackle reached out his arm and hooked Jesse around the neck, bringing him to the ground for a sack—and a loss of five yards.

"Screen pass, forty-five, on three," Jesse said in the huddle. It was the first really cold day of the year, and Jesse was blowing into his hands to keep them warm. "Ready, break!"

On the snap signal, Matt rushed to his left, then cut across the line of scrimmage and headed toward the sideline. He looked over his shoulder, expecting to see the pass. Instead, he saw Jesse being chased down by a South Colby defenseman. The defenseman leaped toward Jesse and grabbed him around the knees.

Just before Jesse hit the ground, he chucked the ball toward Matt. Matt saw the pass wobbling in the air, and skidded to a stop to change direction. The pass was too wide, and a South Colby safety batted it to the ground.

The Panthers had failed to get the first down again. The offense jogged to the sideline and the punting unit ran onto the field.

"I just can't scramble. In fact, with my ankle taped up so much, I can barely move," Jesse said to Matt, as they stood around on the sidelines. "They're sacking me too much. I guess my ankle isn't really ready yet."

"Just worry about your passing," Matt said, blowing into his hands. "It's the front line's job to take care of the South Colby defense."

The spectators in the bleachers were all bundled up in coats and hats and scarves. The wind was blowing so strongly that it lifted Coach's cap from his head and sent it flying beneath the bleachers. All the players along the sidelines were stomping their feet, trying to keep warm.

"Yes!" Josh cried suddenly, pointing out to the field. "Interception!"

Matt spun his head around and saw Chip Simon running with the ball. Chip looked funny with the ball, since he played defense and hardly ever got to carry it. Still, he had snagged the interception, and ran it for thirty-seven yards. He was finally knocked out of bounds at the South Colby twenty-six.

The Panthers had great field position for the first time in the game. The problem was, there were only eight seconds left in the first half. That was only enough time for the Panthers to run one play.

The Panthers lined up. Coach had called for a flag pattern pass to Josh. Matt knew that it would help the Panthers' spirit if they could get some points on the board before halftime. He hoped the Panthers' front line would be able to give Jesse enough time to get the pass off.

Matt ran toward the line, looking to throw a block. Bruce was squared-off with the middle linebacker, blocking him out with his forearms, but the linebacker looked like he was going to break free. Matt tried to throw a block, but the linebacker spun around him, leaving Matt on the ground. The linebacker rushed toward Jesse.

Matt sprang to his feet and ran back across the line of scrimmage, trying to run down the charging linebacker. Jesse scrambled to the side, but the linebacker followed him. Matt couldn't reach the South Colby player in time, and Jesse was forced to throw the ball as he was tackled.

Matt looked up at the pass as it floated through the air. It landed right in the hands of a South Colby pass defender, who happened to be standing in the end zone.

It was a touchback for South Colby, but time ran out before they could run a play. The score at half-time was Colby 7, Alden 0.

Jesse set five yards behind the center, and Matt and Russell split out to the sides as pass receivers. It was the shotgun formation, and Bruce snapped the ball all the way back to Jesse—almost as if Jesse was a punter. Since Jesse was already in the back-field, he was in the perfect position to throw.

It was first down and ten and the Panthers were at the South Colby thirty-two.

Josh was open downfield, and Jesse had enough time to really throw the ball. Matt watched the pass sail high above the defenders' heads, and land right in Josh's arms.

"Yes!" Matt cried, as he watched Josh snag the pass, fake the defense, and run all the way down to the South Colby seventeen.

It had been Matt's idea to have Jesse throw from the shotgun—and it was making all the difference in the second half. Now that Jesse had time to throw, and didn't have to worry about scrambling, he was passing great. The team's confidence suddenly rose to the sky.

"I think we're going to take this game!" Jesse said to Matt before the next huddle.

"All right!" Matt said, slapping Jesse's hand.

The next play was a quarterback option. On the snap signal, Matt ran behind Jesse as Jesse flared out toward the sideline. Jesse had the option to pitch back to Matt or run himself—and that meant that Matt was pretty sure to get the ball.

The safety keyed in on Jesse, so Jesse pitched back to Matt. Matt caught the ball, tucked it into his side, and took off for the end zone. Russell threw a great block in front of him, allowing Matt to dodge toward the center of the field. He could see the defense rushing after him, and turned on the speed. Two safeties were sprinting across the field toward him, trying to stop him before he crossed the goal line. One safety jumped at Matt, knocking his legs out from under him just as he crossed the three-yard line.

Matt flipped through the air. All he hoped was that he would land in the end zone for the touchdown. He crashed to the ground, then looked up to see the referee holding up both arms.

"Touchdown!" the referee cried. Matt jumped up and did his stutter-step dance.

The Panthers now took control of the game. Jesse started from the shotgun on over half of the passing plays, giving him extra time to make a good throw. And he *did* make good throws, one after the other.

At the end of the third quarter, the Panthers were working from a third down on their own forty-nine. Jesse started back in the shotgun, and Josh went long for the bomb. Jesse had all the time he needed, and he waited for Josh to get open far downfield. Matt couldn't believe how long Jesse was waiting. He didn't think Jesse had a chance of throwing the ball that far.

Finally, Jesse took the ball back, and hurled a perfect spiral pass. Josh was three steps ahead of his defender, and all he had to do was look over his shoulder. The ball dropped into his arms, and he kept right on running for an amazing fifty-one-yard touchdown.

The Panthers converted the extra point, bringing the score to Alden 14, South Colby 7, and that was the score when the game ended.

Alden had gotten back their quarterback *and* their

best runningback. Matt felt like the Panthers would be able to beat anybody now—even Williamsport.

Williamsport was already assured of a place in the conference championship, and Matt wanted nothing more than to meet Anderson on the field again.

13

By the next game, Jesse's ankle was feeling almost as strong as ever. His arm was in great shape, too. The work and training that Jesse had done while he was laid up made all the difference. In fact, it almost seemed that he had gotten better at quarterback since his injury.

The game was against Bradley, one of the weakest teams on the Panthers' schedule, and the Panthers drove over them like a steam roller. Bradley's defensive line wasn't strong enough to give Jesse any problems, and he had all the time he needed to throw.

Matt was the first person to mob Jesse when the game ended, with the scoreboard reading Alden 35, Bradley 3.

The last game of the season was against Ellendale, a newcomer to the conference. They were a weak team and it was another easy victory for the Panthers. Jesse was as strong as ever. Matt may not have been running the ball on every play, but whenever he got the ball he made great yardage. By the end of the third quarter, Matt had already gained over one hundred yards, and he was totally psyched. It was the best game he had ever played.

When the final whistle blew, the score was Alden 26, Ellendale 6. The Panthers were headed to the conference championship against Williamsport.

"We did it!" Matt shouted, giving Jesse a sweeping high five as they ran off the field toward the locker rooms. "The Panthers rule!"

"I can't wait for the championship," Jesse answered, smiling. "I can't wait to cream Anderson!"

After the Ellendale victory, Matt, Jesse, Josh, and Russell went to Big Bill's Goal Post for a celebration. Mr. Greene had been at the game, and he wanted to give the boys a special dinner.

"All this football stuff is great," Russell said, gazing around at the pictures on the walls, and the action footage on the televsion screens, and the waiters dressed as referees. "Maybe someday your dad will put *our* picture on the wall. Right beneath the Superbowl teams."

"Let's win the championship first," Matt said, sipping his soda.

The four friends were sitting in a booth right by the biggest video screen, and just then some old footage of Matt's dad flashed on.

"Check it out!" Josh said, pointing to the screen. "It's Mr. Greene. Look at him run."

"He runs like you do, Matt," Russell said. "You have all the same moves."

"I hope Matt runs just like that in the championship," Jesse said.

Matt looked up proudly at the screen. In the footage, Big Bill Greene gave a head fake and sprinted toward open territory. Just when it looked like Big Bill was going to break free for a touchdown, a huge linebacker sped across the field and creamed him. Big Bill fumbled the ball, and the linebacker picked it up for a big turnover.

"Oops," Josh said to Matt, laughing. "Let's just hope you don't run like *that* in the championship."

"Hey, did you guys notice the number of the line-backer who creamed Mr. Greene?" Russell said, lifting his eyebrows. "It was number sixty-six—Anderson's number."

"Wow, that's pretty weird," Jesse said. Jesse was a little bit superstitious, and suddenly he was looking worried. "I hope that doesn't put a jinx on you, Matt."

Matt just laughed. "Come on," he said. "I'm not worried about Anderson."

"Well, the Williamsport game isn't going to be a breeze," Jesse answered. "They're not pushovers. Don't forget, we lost to Williamsport *twice* this year."

Matt pretended that he wasn't fazed. "Now that you're back, and I'm running again, there's nobody who can beat the Panthers," he said confidently.

Deep inside, though, Matt was worried. It was true that Williamsport had beaten the Panthers both times they met. That wasn't a very good record. And Anderson was the kind of player who could get the Williamsport defense totally fired up. Anderson was the also the kind of player who could cause Matt to fumble.

"Uh-oh, look at that," Jesse said, pointing back up to the television screen.

It was the play after Big Bill's fumble, and the

opponents made a beautiful bomb pass for a touch-down. Big Bill's mistake turned into six points for the other side.

"Big deal," Matt said, shrugging. "That game happened fifteen years ago."

"What's everybody looking so down about?" Mr. Greene said, as he strolled up to the boys' booth with another round of sodas. "You're headed to the championships, aren't you?"

"Yeah," Jesse said. "But . . ."

"Then don't let anything get you down," Mr. Greene said. "Take it from me. You can't go into that game just hoping you're going to win. You've got to *know* you're going to win. I'm not saying you should be cocky, or overconfident, but you've got to believe in yourselves."

Everyone nodded. They knew Mr. Greene was right.

14

The day of the championship game was cold and windy, and the sky was a deep blue. There were thin layers of ice on all the puddles in the parking lot and all the leaves had fallen off the trees. In the bleachers, everyone was bundled up in blankets and sipping hot chocolate from steaming cups.

Although it was definitely a cold day outside, things on the playing field were already getting hot.

"That was a late hit," Matt yelled, putting his face

mask right against Anderson's, so that he was shouting into Anderson's face.

"Don't get me mad, Greene," Anderson answered, pushing Matt. "I'm warning you."

"No, I'm warning you," Matt answered, pushing back.

On the last play, Matt had caught a screen pass from Jesse right on the sideline, and his momentum had carried him out of bounds. He had taken at least two steps out of bounds when Anderson wiped him out from the side. Matt was sure it had been a late hit, but the refs didn't drop their flags on the play.

Matt could see the anger in Anderson's blue eyes, and Anderson's face was so red that Matt thought Anderson's helmet might melt. Anderson pushed Matt again, and then the ref stepped in between them.

"Break it up, boys," the ref said, pushing them apart. "You know the rules."

Matt was steaming as he walked back to the huddle. It was only the first quarter, and Anderson was already playing dirty. That was just the kind of play that had gotten Jesse injured.

Matt was glad that the next play was a hand-off.

He couldn't wait to get his hands around that ball, and drive right through Anderson and into the end zone for a touchdown.

The Panthers were on the Williamsport forty-two, and it was second down with seven yards to go. The score was 0–0, but Matt had plans to change that soon.

"Hut, hut!"

Matt got the hand-off and checked out the situation. Russell was running in front of him in an attempt to block Anderson. But Matt watched as Anderson swept Russell aside and ran right into Matt's path. Matt tried to dodge around him, but Anderson was too fast on his feet. Matt jumped into the air and felt Anderson's arms surround his waist and pull him to the ground.

After hearing the whistle, Matt dropped the ball and lay on his back, trying to catch his breath. He wasn't mad at Anderson. The play was fair. He was mad at himself for not cutting around Anderson, or breaking free of the tackle.

Now the Panthers had lost a yard. It was third down and seven.

"Screen, forty-five left, on three," Jesse said in the huddle. "Break."

Matt had to get a first down on this screen pass,

or the Panthers would have to punt. Jesse had been passing well so far, so Matt was pretty sure Jesse would get the ball to him. After that, it was up to Matt to make things happen.

On the snap signal, Matt burst left and crossed the line of scrimmage. He saw Anderson fade left to cover him, and then turned his head around for the pass.

Jesse had thrown a beauty, and Matt snatched it with both hands, tucked it in, and cut upfield. Anderson was steaming across the grass toward Matt, and another Williamsport linebacker was running toward him along the sideline. He was trapped on all sides, so he decided to cut right and try to spin around Anderson.

Anderson was waiting for him, and Matt felt Anderson's shoulder pad crush into his stomach. The ball jarred loose from his arms on the tackle, and fell to the ground just as Anderson fell on top of Matt. When he hit the ground, Matt felt a sharp pain in his ribs and let out a yell.

The other Williamsport linebacker picked up Matt's fumble, and ran it all the way to the Alden thirty-four. When the ref blew his whistle and called the play dead, Matt was still lying on the field, holding his ribs.

Coach Litzinger ran out and knelt down beside Matt.

"It's my side," Matt said. "It feels bruised or something."

Matt couldn't believe he was hurt. This was the most important game of his life, and he couldn't stand the thought of missing any of the action. Coach and Jesse helped Matt to his feet, and Matt walked slowly to the sidelines. After a few moments, he touched his side. It hurt, but he was certain that nothing was broken.

"I want to go back in, Coach," Matt said. "My ribs are fine."

"Sorry, Matt," Coach answered. "I've called ahead for the Emergency Room. You're going to the hospital and we'll have to wait and see what they say about your ribs."

"The hospital?" Matt cried. "How long is that going to take?"

"I don't know," Coach said. "I'd like to have you playing, too. But nobody plays if they're hurt. Period."

Matt took a deep breath and watched the Williamsport offense line up.

Mr. Greene came down from the stands to take Matt to the hospital. As they walked toward the parking lot Matt looked over his shoulder to see the Williamsport quarterback fading back for a pass. The Panthers' defense was putting good pressure on him and Matt stopped walking to cheer them on. Just when the quarterback was about to be sacked, he got off a perfect throw to the wide receiver, who was cutting across the end zone.

The wide receiver caught the pass for the first touchdown of the game.

"Come on, Matt," Mr. Greene said. "The quicker we get you checked out, the quicker you can get back in there."

Matt heard the crowd cheering as he opened the door of his dad's car. Somehow he knew that Williamsport had scored again.

15

Ten minutes later, Mr. Greene pulled into the Emergency Room at the Cranbrook Hospital, and Matt jumped out of the car. He ran at top speed up to the reception desk, and told the nurse he needed an X-ray.

"*As fast as possible,*" Matt added. "It's *very* important. I'm in the middle of a game, the championship game!"

The nurse said Matt would just have to wait like everyone else. Matt couldn't believe what was happening. The Panthers were playing a championship game, and *he* was sitting in a stupid hospital.

"Let's see," Matt said impatiently, checking the clock on the wall. "The second half has probably just started. I hope the Panthers are doing better."

A nurse finally led Matt into a room with a big X-ray machine. Matt took off his shirt and laid down on a gray table. A doctor came in and lowered the X-ray machine over Matt's chest, lined it up, then left the room. A moment later, he came back in and told Matt to wait in his office.

"How long until you know?" Matt asked.

"It takes some time to develop the X-rays," the doctor answered. "Believe me, Matt. If everything's okay, I'll get you out of here as fast as I can."

"But the third quarter is almost over," Matt said.

Matt was tempted to dart out of the hospital and sprint all the way back to the field, but he knew if he did that he would be too exhausted to play.

"Good news, Matt," the doctor said after about fifteen minutes. "Your ribs are fine."

"I told you!" Matt said, jumping to his feet and grabbing Mr. Greene's sleeve. "Let's get going!"

Matt jumped out of the car and ran as fast as he could back toward the Panthers' sideline.

When he looked up to the scoreboard, his heart sank.

It was Williamsport 14, Alden 0—and there was only a minute and forty-eight seconds left in the game. Things were looking bad for the Panthers.

"I'm back, Coach!" Matt said. "The doctor says I can play."

"Great! We sure need you," Coach said. "You can run in with the next play."

It was third down and six, and the Panthers were on the Williamsport thirty-six. Coach told Matt the next play was going to be a pitch-out, and Matt jogged onto the field.

When Jesse, Bruce, Josh, Russell, and the rest of the offense saw Matt jogging out, they let out a cheer and started clapping. Matt was psyched. He looked over toward Anderson and smiled. He didn't think Anderson had a chance to stop him now.

"Hut, hut!"

Matt flared out to his right, and watched as Jesse pitched him the football. He grabbed the ball and his instincts took over. He scanned the field and cut across the line of scrimmage. Anderson followed him across, but Matt faked left and cut right, leaving Anderson on the ground.

Then Matt turned on the speed. He spun out of a

tackle, then turned toward the far flag and cut across the field. Matt's legs carried him faster and faster. He kept his eyes focused on the goal line until he crossed it all alone.

The Alden fans went crazy.

Matt tossed the ball to the ref, then did his famous touchdown dance—which made the crowd cheer even louder. Matt felt great, but he knew the Panthers were still behind, and there was only a minute and thirty-two seconds left in the game.

The Panthers decided to go for the extra point. Duke's kick was good. The score was now 14–7.

"Great run, Matt," Coach said on the sidelines, as the team gathered around. "Now, listen up, men. There are less than two minutes left in the game. If we let Williamsport keep the ball, they can just kill the clock and the game is theirs. We have to get possession of the ball. So we're going to try an onside kick."

The Panthers had never tried an onside kick in a game, but they didn't have much choice.

"Okay, men," Coach said. "I know you can do it. Let's go!"

Matt watched from the sidelines as the kick-off team lined up. Williamsport was ready for the onside kick, and as soon as Duke kicked the ball the Williamsport front line scrambled forward. Matt watched as the Panthers ran after the ball, which was bouncing crazily along the ground. A huge mass of players fell on the ball, and Matt couldn't tell which side had gained possession.

Matt held his breath as the players got up from the pile. Finally the referee pointed toward the Alden end zone and the Panthers went crazy. They had regained possession!

But they only had a minute and twenty-two seconds to score. Coach called for a pitch-out to Matt.

Matt knew that if he stayed in bounds, the clock would keep running and the Panthers would lose precious seconds. So on the snap signal, Matt got the pitch-out and headed for the sidelines.

Anderson was on him all the way, and Matt couldn't make it to the sideline before Anderson took him out. He had gained two yards but the clock was still ticking. It was second and eight. Since there wasn't enough time to bring a play in from Coach, Jesse had to call the play himself.

"Screen pass, forty-five left, on three," Jesse said, looking at Matt. "Break."

Matt lined up behind Jesse and took off to the left on the signal. When he crossed the line of scrimmage, he looked back for the pass. The ball was speeding in a perfect spiral, and Matt snatched it, then turned upfield. He kept one eye on the sideline to make sure he could get there. Suddenly his legs got cut out from under him, and he went flying through the air.

Matt hit the ground hard, but he was fine. He was just angry that he wasn't able to get out of bounds again.

"You don't look so hot," Anderson said as Matt hurried to his feet. "I guess the Panthers don't have what it takes to win."

Matt didn't have time to answer. The clock was still ticking down. Jesse called for a long play-action post pattern pass to Josh, and when the huddle broke there were only twenty-three seconds left in the game.

"Hut, hut!"

Matt rushed forward for the play-action fake hand-off. Jesse put the ball in his stomach, then pulled it out, and Matt went barreling into the Williamsport defense. But Anderson wasn't fooled. Instead of rushing to tackle Matt, Anderson turned and sprinted across the field toward Josh.

Matt broke a tackle, twisted free, and ran downfield. He turned to watch Jesse throw the ball, heaving it high in the air. Anderson was catching up to Josh and both players looked over their shoulders to see the pass come closer and closer.

The pass was perfect and Anderson couldn't get his hands on it. Josh leapt into the air and caught the ball. Matt cheered as he watched Josh cross the goal line with Anderson tagging along just behind.

But when Josh slowed down and lifted his arms in triumph, Anderson dove forward and smashed him in the side. The referees' flags were flying, even before Josh hit the ground and skidded to a stop. Anderson landed on top of Josh, shoved him once, and then got up angrily to face the refs' whistles. Matt had never seen such an obvious case of a late hit, and he was glad that this time the refs had caught Anderson red-handed.

Matt watched the referees huddle near the goal line. Anderson was standing with his hands on his hips, looking cocky. Finally the huddle of refs broke up and the crowd quieted to hear the call. "Late hit, unsportsmanlike conduct, number sixty-six," the head ref called out, making the hand motions as well. "The player is ejected from the game."

"Yes," Matt said, smiling as the Alden crowd began to cheer.

Paste

Anderson walked toward Matt. "It doesn't matter. You guys are going to lose anyway."

Matt didn't respond. He jogged back to the Panthers sideline and looked at the scoreboard. The score was now Williamsport 14, Alden 13.

There were only two seconds left on the clock.

"What do you think we're going to do?" Jesse asked Matt.

"I don't know," Matt answered. "With Anderson out of the game, I hope we go for the two-point conversion."

Matt thought about the situation. Duke was a good kicker, and they had a good chance of scoring the extra point. That would tie the game, and take it into overtime. Or, the Panthers could go for the two-point conversion. If they scored, they would get two points and win the championship. If they didn't get the conversion, they'd lose the championship.

"We're going for the conversion," Coach said. "Pitch-out, forty-five, right. On three."

Matt felt his heart began to pound. He knew all the pressure was on him. The whole season came down to this play.

"Hey, Matt," Coach said before the team ran out. "I know you can do it."

"I will, Coach," Matt answered.

Matt had never been more nervous as he got down in the three point stance and waited for the snap signal.

"Ready!" Jesse cried. "Hut, hut, hut!"

Matt burst forward, flared to the right, and looked for the pitch-out. Jesse pitched the ball right into his hands, and Matt turned toward the goal line. The first thing he saw was a linebacker charging forward. That's when Matt made his decision. He leaped up high, just as the linebacker dived low for his belt buckle. Matt soared right over the linebacker's head and tumbled into the end zone.

He didn't even have a chance to get to his feet before the Panthers team mobbed him. The next thing he knew, Matt was being lifted up onto the shoulders of his teammates, and the crowd was going crazy. Matt turned to the Williamsport sideline and caught one last glimpse of Anderson, just as Anderson smashed his helmet to the ground in frustration. Matt lifted up his arms and let out an enormous yell.

The Alden Panthers were the champs.

Pro Set Cards
and the
Alden All Stars
present
THE ALL STAR SWEEPSTAKES

- **Grand Prize: a trip for two to the 1992 Pro Bowl in Hawaii**

- **First Prize: a *complete* set of Pro Set's 1991 Series I and II—the *official* card of the NFL. Complete sets are not available in stores.**

- **Two Second Prizes: all of the books in the Alden All Stars series—nine books in all!**

OFFICIAL RULES—NO PURCHASE NECESSARY

1. On an official entry form, print your name, address, zip code, and age. Use the entry form printed below, or you may obtain an entry form and a set of rules by sending a self-addressed stamped envelope to: ALL STAR SWEEPSTAKES, P.O. Box 655, Sayreville, NJ 08871. Residents of WA and VT need not include return postage. Requests must be received by October 15, 1991.

2. Enter as often as you wish, but each entry must be mailed separately to ALL STAR SWEEPSTAKES, P.O. Box 516, Sayreville, NJ 08871. No mechanically reproduced entries will be accepted. All entries must be received by November 30, 1991.

3. Winners will be selected from among all eligible entries received, in a random drawing conducted by Marden-Kane Inc., an independent judging organization whose decisions are final in all matters relating to this sweepstakes. All prizes will be awarded and winners notified by mail. Prizes are nontransferable, and no substitutions or cash equivalents are allowed. Taxes, if any, are the responsibility of the winners. Winners may be asked to execute an affidavit of eligibility and release. No responsibility is assumed for lost or misdirected mail. Grand Prize consists of a four-night/five-day trip for two to the 1992 Pro Bowl in Hawaii, including round-trip air transportation, hotel accommodations, game tickets, hotel-to-game and hotel-to-airport transfers, breakfasts and dinners. In the event that the trip is won by a minor, it will be awarded in the name of a parent or legal guardian. Trip must be taken on date specified or the prize will be forfeited and an alternate winner selected. Approximate retail value of the Grand Prize is $3500. First Prize consists of a complete set of Pro Set's 1991 series I and II football cards. Pro Set cards are the official card of the NFL and complete sets are not available in stores. Two second prizes consist of a complete set of the Alden All Stars series, constituting nine books as of the time of the drawing. Approximate retail value of each of the Second Prizes is $50. PENGUIN USA and its affiliates reserve the right to use the prize winners' names and likenesses in any promotional activities relating to this sweepstakes without further compensation to the winners.

4. This Sweepstakes is open to residents of the U.S. only. Employees and their families of PENGUIN USA and its affiliates, advertising/promotion agencies, and retailers, and employees of Daniel Weiss Associates, Inc. may not enter. This offer is void wherever prohibited and subject to all federal, state, and local laws. NFL Properties is not a sponsor nor endorses this sweepstakes.

5. For a list of winners, send a stamped, self-addressed envelope to ALL STAR SWEEPSTAKES WINNERS, P.O. Box 705, Sayreville, NJ 08871.

ALL STAR SWEEPSTAKES OFFICIAL ENTRY FORM

Name _____ Age _____

Address _____

City/State/ZIP _____

(please print)